THE FLYING SAUCER
CAME DOWN VERTICALLY
THROUGH THE CLOUDS,
BRAKED TO A HALT ABOUT
FIFTY FEET FROM THE
GROUND, AND SETTLED
WITH A CONSIDERABLE
BUMP ON A PATCH OF
HEATHER-STREWN
MOORLAND.

"That," said Captain Wyxtpthll, "was a lousy landing." He did not, of course, use precisely these words. To human ears his remarks would have sounded rather like the clucking of an angry hen.

Master Pilot Krtclugg unwound three of his tentacles from the control panel, stretched all four of his legs, and relaxed comfortably.

"Not my fault the automatics have packed up again," he grumbled. "But what do you expect with a ship that should have been scrapped five thousand years ago?"

—From *Trouble with The Natives*

"THIS VOLUME PRESENTS AN EXCELLENT CROSS-SECTION OF ONE OF SCIENCE-FICTION'S FOREMOST EXPONENTS!"
—*Galaxy Magazine*

By Arthur C. Clarke
Published by Ballantine Books:

REACH
for
TOMORROW

Arthur C. Clarke

A Del Rey Book

BALLANTINE BOOKS • NEW YORK

To Scott Meredith
for selling all these stories at least once.

Preface

Preface writing is an occupational disease of authors, but it must be granted that they have a legitimate excuse. It is the only opportunity they ever get of pinning their readers into a corner and telling them exactly what they are trying to do. In my case, this can be stated very briefly. I wrote these stories to entertain one person—myself. It still seems a remarkabe piece of good luck to me that other people have been entertained as well.

"Rescue Party," which was written in 1945, was my first published story, and a depressing number of people still consider it my best. If this is indeed the case, I have been steadily going downhill for the past ten years, and those who continue to praise this story will understand why my gratitude is so well controlled. Readers of my earlier collection, EXPEDITION TO EARTH, may just conceivably be interested in knowing that "History Lesson" and "Rescue Party" both stemmed from the same forgotten original, though now it would be difficult to find two more contrasting endings.

It seems only right to warn the reader that "Jupiter Five," "Technical Error" and "The Fires Within" are all pure science fiction. In each case some unfamiliar (but I hope both plausible and comprehensible) scientific fact is the basis of the story action, and human interest is secondary. Some critics maintain that this is always a Bad Thing; I believe this is too sweeping a generalization. In his perceptive preface to A. D. 2500, for example, Mr. Angus Wilson remarks: "Science fiction which ends as technical information dressed with a little fantasy or plot can never be any good." But any good for what? If it is done properly, without the information being too obtrusive or redolent of the textbook, it can still have at least the entertainment value of a good puzzle. It may not be art, but it can be enjoyable and intriguing.

I am by no means sure that I could write "Jupiter Five" today; it involved twenty or thirty pages of orbital calculations and should by rights be dedicated to Professor G. C. McVittie, my erstwhile tutor in applied mathematics. (I had better hasten to add that he bears no slightest resemblance to the professor in the story.) This fact is mentioned, not to boast of now forgotten skills, nor to scare nervous readers whose maths stopped at the multiplication table, but to make it clear that the surprising state of affairs described in the story really exists, and is not a figment of my imagination. What is more, it exists not only in the remote orbit of Jupiter V but will soon do so, much closer to home, among the artificial satellites of the next decade.

"Time's Arrow" is an example of how hard it is for the science-fiction writer to keep ahead of fact. The quite —at the time the story was written—imaginary discovery described in the tale now actually exists, and may be seen in the New York Natural History Museum. I think it most unlikely, however, that the rest of the story will ever come true. . . .

"The Forgotten Enemy" also involved a geological—or perhaps one should say meteorological—theme. I apologize in advance to any experts who may be offended by the slight liberties I have taken with time-scales. But what is a factor of 10^3 among friends?

"The Curse" now appears, perhaps, somewhat less imaginative than when it was first published in the distant dawn of the Atomic Age, before tritium had succeeded uranium and the wheel had gone full circle to uranium again. It was written within a few miles of the small and famous slab of stone whose ultimate fate it describes.

To the best of my recollection (and like most authors I am singularly bad at remembering this sort of thing) I have written only two stories based on ideas suggested by other people. One of them is "The Possessed," and I hereby acknowledge my thanks to Mike Wilson, who can take his share of any blame.

Arthur C. Clarke

Contents

Rescue Party

WHO WAS TO BLAME? FOR THREE DAYS ALVERON'S THOUGHTS had come back to that question, and still he had found no answer. A creature of a less civilized or a less sensitive race would never have let it torture his mind, and would have satisfied himself with the assurance that no one could be responsible for the working of fate. But Alveron and his kind had been lords of the Universe since the dawn of history, since that far distant age when the Time Barrier had been folded round the cosmos by the unknown powers that lay beyond the Beginning. To them had been given all knowledge—and with infinite knowledge went infinite responsibility. If there were mistakes and errors in the administration of the galaxy, the fault lay on the heads of Alveron and his people. And this was no mere mistake: it was one of the greatest tragedies in history.

The crew still knew nothing. Even Rugon, his closest friend and the ship's deputy captain, had been told only part of the truth. But now the doomed worlds lay less than a billion miles ahead. In a few hours, they would be landing on the third planet.

Once again Alveron read the message from Base; then, with a flick of a tentacle that no human eye could have followed, he pressed the "General Attention" button. Throughout the mile-long cylinder that was the Galactic Survey Ship S9000, creatures of many races laid down their work to listen to the words of their captain.

"I know you have all been wondering," began Alveron, "why we were ordered to abandon our survey and to proceed at such an acceleration to this region of space. Some of you may realize what this acceleration means. Our ship is on its last voyage: the generators have already been running for sixty hours at Ultimate Overload. We

1

will be very lucky if we return to Base under our own power.

"We are approaching a sun which is about to become a Nova. Detonation will occur in seven hours, with an uncertainty of one hour, leaving us a maximum of only four hours for exploration. There are ten planets in the system about to be destroyed—and there is a civilization on the third. That fact was discovered only a few days ago. It is our tragic mission to contact that doomed race and if possible to save some of its members. I know that there is little we can do in so short a time with this single ship. No other machine can possibly reach the system before detonation occurs."

There was a long pause during which there could have been no sound or movement in the whole of the mighty ship as it sped silently toward the worlds ahead. Alveron knew what his companions were thinking and he tried to answer their unspoken question.

"You will wonder how such a disaster, the greatest of which we have any record, has been allowed to occur. On one point I can reassure you. The fault does not lie with the Survey.

"As you know, with our present fleet of under twelve thousand ships, it is possible to re-examine each of the eight thousand million solar systems in the Galaxy at intervals of about a million years. Most worlds change very little in so short a time as that.

"Less than four hundred thousand years ago, the survey ship S5060 examined the planets of the system we are approaching. It found intelligence on none of them, though the third planet was teeming with animal life and two other worlds had once been inhabited. The usual report was submitted and the system is due for its next examination in six hundred thousand years.

"It now appears that in the incredibly short period since the last survey, intelligent life has appeared in the system. The first intimation of this occurred when unknown radio signals were detected on the planet Kulath in the system X29.35, Y34.76, Z27.93. Bearings were taken on them; they were coming from the system ahead.

"Kulath is two hundred light-years from here, so those radio waves had been on their way for two centuries. Thus for at least that period of time a civilization has existed on one of these worlds—a civilization that can generate electromagnetic waves and all that that implies.

"An immediate telescopic examination of the system was made and it was then found that the sun was in the unstable pre-nova stage. Detonation might occur at any moment, and indeed might have done so while the light waves were on their way to Kulath.

"There was a slight delay while the supervelocity scanners on Kulath II were focused on to the system. They showed that the explosion had not yet occurred but was only a few hours away. If Kulath had been a fraction of a light-year further from this sun, we should never have known of its civilization until it had ceased to exist.

"The Administrator of Kulath contacted Sector Base immediately, and I was ordered to proceed to the system at once. Our object is to save what members we can of the doomed race, if indeed there are any left. But we have assumed that a civilization possessing radio could have protected itself against any rise of temperature that may have already occurred.

"This ship and the two tenders will each explore a section of the planet. Commander Torkalee will take Number One, Commander Orostron Number Two. They will have just under four hours in which to explore this world. At the end of that time, they must be back in the ship. It will be leaving then, with or without them. I will give the two commanders detailed instructions in the control room immediately.

"That is all. We enter atmosphere in two hours."

On the world once known as Earth the fires were dying out: there was nothing left to burn. The great forests that had swept across the planet like a tidal wave with the passing of the cities were now no more than glowing charcoal and the smoke of their funeral pyres still stained the sky. But the last hours were still to come, for the surface rocks had not yet begun to flow. The continents were dimly visible through the haze, but their outlines meant nothing to the watchers in the approaching ship. The charts they possessed were out of date by a dozen Ice Ages and more deluges than one.

The S9000 had driven past Jupiter and seen at once that no life could exist in those half-gaseous oceans of compressed hydrocarbons, now erupting furiously under the sun's abnormal heat. Mars and the outer planets they had missed, and Alveron realized that the worlds nearer the sun than Earth would be already melting. It was more than likely, he thought sadly, that the tragedy of this unknown race was already finished. Deep in his heart, he thought it might be better so. The ship could only have carried a few hundred survivors, and the problem of selection had been haunting his mind.

Rugon, Chief of Communications and Deputy Captain, came into the control room. For the last hour he had been striving to detect radiation from Earth, but in vain.

"We're too late," he announced gloomily. "I've monitored the whole spectrum and the ether's dead except for our own stations and some two-hundred-year-old programs from Kulath. Nothing in this system is radiating any more."

He moved toward the giant vision screen with a graceful flowing motion that no mere biped could ever hope to imitate. Alveron said nothing; he had been expecting this news.

One entire wall of the control room was taken up by the screen, a great black rectangle that gave an impression of almost infinite depth. Three of Rugon's slender control tentacles, useless for heavy work but incredibly swift at all manipulation, flickered over the selector dials and the screen lit up with a thousand points of light. The star field flowed swiftly past as Rugon adjusted the controls, bringing the projector to bear upon the sun itself.

No man of Earth would have recognized the monstrous shape that filled the screen. The sun's light was white no longer: great violet-blue clouds covered half its surface and from them long streamers of flame were erupting into space. At one point an enormous prominence had reared itself out of the photosphere, far out even into the flickering veils of the corona. It was as though a tree of fire had taken root in the surface of the sun—a tree that stood half a million miles high and whose branches were rivers of flame sweeping through space at hundreds of miles a second.

"I suppose," said Rugon presently, "that you are quite satisfied about the astronomers' calculations. After all——"

"Oh, we're perfectly safe," said Alveron confidently. "I've spoken to Kulath Observatory and they have been making some additional checks through our own instruments. That uncertainty of an hour includes a private safety margin which they won't tell me in case I feel tempted to stay any longer."

He glanced at the instrument board.

"The pilot should have brought us to the atmosphere now. Switch the screen back to the planet, please. Ah, there they go!"

There was a sudden tremor underfoot and a raucous clanging of alarms, instantly stilled. Across the vision screen two slim projectiles dived toward the looming mass of Earth. For a few miles they traveled together, then they separated, one vanishing abruptly as it entered the shadow of the planet.

Slowly the huge mother ship, with its thousand times greater mass, descended after them into the raging storms that already were tearing down the deserted cities of Man.

It was night in the hemisphere over which Orostron drove his tiny command. Like Torkalee, his mission was to photograph and record, and to report progress to the mother ship. The little scout had no room for specimens or passengers. If contact was made with the inhabitants of this world, the S9000 would come at once. There would be no time for parleying. If there was any trouble the rescue would be by force and the explanations could come later.

The ruined land beneath was bathed with an eerie, flickering light, for a great auroral display was raging over half the world. But the image on the vision screen was independent of external light, and it showed clearly a waste of barren rock that seemed never to have known any form of life. Presumably this desert land must come to an end somewhere. Orostron increased his speed to the highest value he dared risk in so dense an atmosphere.

The machine fled on through the storm, and presently the desert of rock began to climb toward the sky. A great mountain range lay ahead, its peaks lost in the smoke-laden clouds. Orostron directed the scanners toward the horizon, and on the vision screen the line of mountains seemed suddenly very close and menacing. He started to climb rapidly. It was difficult to imagine a more unpromising land in which to find civilization and he wondered if it would be wise to change course. He decided against it. Five minutes later, he had his reward.

Miles below lay a decapitated mountain, the whole of its summit sheared away by some tremendous feat of engineering. Rising out of the rock and straddling the artificial plateau was an intricate structure of metal girders, supporting masses of machinery. Orostron brought his ship to a halt and spiraled down toward the mountain.

The slight Doppler blur had now vanished, and the picture on the screen was clear-cut. The latticework was supporting some scores of great metal mirrors, pointing skyward at an angle of forty-five degrees to the horizontal. They were slightly concave, and each had some complicated mechanism at its focus. There seemed something impressive and purposeful about the great array; every mirror was aimed at precisely the same spot in the sky— or beyond.

Orostron turned to his colleagues.

"It looks like some kind of observatory to me," he said. "Have you ever seen anything like it before?"

Klarten, a multitentacled, tripedal creature from a globular cluster at the edge of the Milky Way, had a different theory.

"That's communication equipment. Those reflectors are for focusing electromagnetic beams. I've seen the same kind of installation on a hundred worlds before. It may even be the station that Kulath picked up—though that's rather unlikely, for the beams would be very narrow from mirrors that size."

"That would explain why Rugon could detect no radiation before we landed," added Hansur II, one of the twin beings from the planet Thargon.

Orostron did not agree at all.

"If that is a radio station, it must be built for interplanetary communication. Look at the way the mirrors are pointed. I don't believe that a race which has only had radio for two centuries can have crossed space. It took my people six thousand years to do it."

"We managed it in three," said Hansur II mildly, speaking a few seconds ahead of his twin. Before the inevitable argument could develop, Klarten began to wave his tentacles with excitement. While the others had been talking, he had started the automatic monitor.

"Here it is! Listen!"

He threw a switch, and the little room was filled with a raucous whining sound, continually changing in pitch but nevertheless retaining certain characteristics that were difficult to define.

The four explorers listened intently for a minute; then Orostron said, "Surely that can't be any form of speech! No creature could produce sounds as quickly as that!"

Hansur I had come to the same conclusion. "That's a television program. Don't you think so, Klarten?"

The other agreed.

"Yes, and each of those mirrors seems to be radiating a different program. I wonder where they're going? If I'm correct, one of the other planets in the system must lie along those beams. We can soon check that."

Orostron called the S9000 and reported the discovery. Both Rugon and Alveron were greatly excited, and made a quick check of the astronomical records.

The result was surprising—and disappointing. None of the other nine planets lay anywhere near the line of transmission. The great mirrors appeared to be pointing blindly into space.

There seemed only one conclusion to be drawn, and Klarten was the first to voice it.

"They had interplanetary communication," he said. "But the station must be deserted now, and the transmitters no longer controlled. They haven't been switched off, and are just pointing where they were left."

"Well, we'll soon find out," said Orostron. "I'm going to land."

He brought the machine slowly down to the level of the great metal mirrors, and past them until it came to rest on the mountain rock. A hundred yards away, a white stone building crouched beneath the maze of steel girders. It was windowless, but there were several doors in the wall facing them.

Orostron watched his companions climb into their protective suits and wished he could follow. But someone had to stay in the machine to keep in touch with the mother ship. Those were Alveron's instructions, and they were very wise. One never knew what would happen on a world that was being explored for the first time, especially under conditions such as these.

Very cautiously, the three explorers stepped out of the airlock and adjusted the antigravity field of their suits. Then, each with the mode of locomotion peculiar to his race, the little party went toward the building, the Hansur twins leading and Klarten following close behind. His gravity control was apparently giving trouble, for he suddenly fell to the ground, rather to the amusement of his colleagues. Orostron saw them pause for a moment at the nearest door—then it opened slowly and they disappeared from sight.

So Orostron waited, with what patience he could, while the storm rose around him and the light of the aurora grew even brighter in the sky. At the agreed times he called the mother ship and received brief acknowledgments from Rugon. He wondered how Torkalee was faring, halfway round the planet, but he could not contact him through the crash and thunder of solar interference.

It did not take Klarten and the Hansurs long to discover that their theories were largely correct. The building was a radio station, and it was utterly deserted. It consisted of one tremendous room with a few small offices leading from it. In the main chamber, row after row of electrical equipment stretched into the distance; lights flickered and winked on hundreds of control panels, and a dull glow came from the elements in a great avenue of vacuum tubes.

But Klarten was not impressed. The first radio set his race had built were now fossilized in strata a thousand million years old. Man, who had possessed electrical machines for only a few centuries, could not compete with those who had known them for half the lifetime of the Earth.

Nevertheless, the party kept their recorders running as they explored the building. There was still one problem to be solved. The deserted station was broadcasting programs, but where were they coming from? The central switchboard had been quickly located. It was designed to handle scores of programs simultaneously, but the source of those programs was lost in a maze of cables that vanished underground. Back in the S9000, Rugon was trying to analyze the broadcasts and perhaps his researches would reveal their origin. It was impossible to trace cables that might lead across continents.

The party wasted little time at the deserted station. There was nothing they could learn from it, and they were seeking life rather than scientific information. A few minutes later the little ship rose swiftly from the plateau and headed toward the plains that must lie beyond the mountains. Less than three hours were still left to them.

As the array of enigmatic mirrors dropped out of sight, Orostron was struck by a sudden thought. Was it imagination, or had they all moved through a small angle while he had been waiting, as if they were still compensating for the rotation of the Earth? He could not be sure, and he dismissed the matter as unimportant. It would only mean that the directing mechanism was still working, after a fashion.

They discovered the city fifteen minutes later. It was a great, sprawling metropolis, built around a river that had disappeared leaving an ugly scar winding its way among the great buildings and beneath bridges that looked very incongruous now.

Even from the air, the city looked deserted. But only two and a half hours were left—there was no time for further exploration. Orostron made his decision, and landed near the largest structure he could see. It seemed reasonable to suppose that some creatures would have sought shelter in the strongest buildings, where they would be safe until the very end.

The deepest caves—the heart of the planet itself—would give no protection when the final cataclysm came. Even if this race had reached the outer planets, its doom would only be delayed by the few hours it would take for the ravening wavefronts to cross the Solar System.

Orostron could not know that the city had been deserted not for a few days or weeks, but for over a century. For the culture of cities, which had outlasted so many civilizations had been doomed at last when the helicopter brought universal transportation. Within a few generations the great masses of mankind, knowing that they could reach any part of the globe in a matter of hours, had gone back to the fields and forests for which they had always longed. The new civilization had machines and resources of which earlier ages had never dreamed, but it was essentially rural and no longer bound to the steel and concrete warrens that had dominated the centuries before. Such cities as still remained were specialized centers of research, administration or entertainment; the others had been allowed to decay, where it was too much trouble to destroy them. The dozen or so greatest of all cities, and the ancient university towns, had scarcely changed and would have lasted for many generations to come. But the cities that had been founded on steam and iron and surface transportation had passed with the industries that had nourished them.

And so while Orostron waited in the tender, his colleagues raced through endless empty corridors and deserted halls, taking innumerable photographs but learning nothing of the creatures who had used these buildings. There were libraries, meeting places, council rooms, thousands of offices—all were empty and deep with dust. If they had not seen the radio station on its mountain eyrie, the explorers could well have believed that this world had known no life for centuries.

Through the long minutes of waiting, Orostron tried to imagine where this race could have vanished. Perhaps they had killed themselves knowing that escape was impossible; perhaps they had built great shelters in the bowels of the planet, and even now were cowering in their millions beneath his feet, waiting for the end. He began to fear that he would never know.

It was almost a relief when at last he had to give the order for the return. Soon he would know if Torkalee's party had been more fortunate. And he was anxious to get back to the mother ship, for as the minutes passed the suspense had become more and more acute. There had always been the thought in his mind: What if the astronomers of Kulath have made a mistake? He would begin to feel happy when the walls of the S9000 were around him. He would be happier still when they were out in space and this ominous sun was shrinking far astern.

As soon as his colleagues had entered the airlock, Orostron hurled his tiny machine into the sky and set the controls to home on the S9000. Then he turned to his friends.

"Well, what have you found?" he asked.

Klarten produced a large roll of canvas and spread it out on the floor.

"This is what they were like," he said quietly. "Bipeds, with only two arms. They seem to have managed well, in spite of that handicap. Only two eyes as well, unless there are others in the back. We were lucky to find this; it's about the only thing they left behind."

The ancient oil paintings stared stonily back at the three creatures regarding it so intently. By the irony of fate, its complete worthlessness had saved it from oblivion. When the city had been evacuated, no one had bothered to move Alderman John Richards, 1909-1974. For a century and a half he had been gathering dust while far away from the old cities the new civilization had been rising to heights no earlier culture had ever known.

"That was almost all we found," said Klarten. "The city must have been deserted for years. I'm afraid our expedition has been a failure. If there are any living beings on this world, they've hidden themselves too well for us to find them."

His commander was forced to agree.

"It was an almost impossible task," he said. "If we'd had weeks instead of hours we might have succeeded. For all we know, they may even have built shelters under the sea. No one seems to have thought of that."

He glanced quickly at the indicators and corrected the course.

"We'll be there in five minutes. Alveron seems to be moving rather quickly. I wonder if Torkalee has found anything."

The S9000 was hanging a few miles above the seaboard of a blazing continent when Orostron homed upon it. The danger line was thirty minutes away and there was no time to lose. Skillfully, he maneuvered the little ship into its launching tube and the party stepped out of the airlock.

There was a small crowd waiting for them. That was to be expected, but Orostron could see at once that something more than curiosity had brought his friends here. Even before a word was spoken, he knew that something was wrong.

"Torkalee hasn't returned. He's lost his party and we're going to the rescue. Come along to the control room at once."

From the beginning, Torkalee had been luckier than Orostron. He had followed the zone of twilight, keeping away from the intolerable glare of the sun, until he came to the shores of an inland sea. It was a very recent sea, one of the latest of Man's works, for the land it covered had been desert less than a century before. In a few hours it would be desert again, for the water was boiling and clouds of steam were rising to the skies. But they could not veil the loveliness of the great white city that overlooked the tideless sea.

Flying machines were still parked neatly round the

square in which Torkalee landed. They were disappointingly primitive, though beautifully finished, and depended on rotating airfoils for support. Nowhere was there any sign of life, but the place gave the impression that its inhabitants were not very far away. Lights were still shining from some of the windows.

Torkalee's three companions lost no time in leaving the machine. Leader of the party, by seniority of rank and race was T'sinadree, who like Alveron himself had been born on one of the ancient planets of the Central Suns. Next came Alarkane, from a race which was one of the youngest in the Universe and took a perverse pride in the fact. Last came one of the strange beings from the system of Palador. It was nameless, like all its kind, for it possessed no identity of its own, being merely a mobile but still dependent cell in the consciousness of its race. Though it and its fellows had long been scattered over the galaxy in the exploration of countless worlds, some unknown link still bound them together as inexorably as the living cells in a human body.

When a creature of Palador spoke, the pronoun it used was always "We." There was not, nor could there ever be, any first person singular in the language of Palador.

The great doors of the splendid building baffled the explorers, though any human child would have known their secret. T'sinadree wasted no time on them but called Torkalee on his personal transmitter. Then the three hurried aside while their commander maneuvered his machine into the best position. There was a brief burst of intolerable flame; the massive steelwork flickered once at the edge of the visible spectrum and was gone. The stones were still glowing when the eager party hurried into the building, the beams of their light projectors fanning before them.

The torches were not needed. Before them lay a great hall, glowing with light from lines of tubes along the ceiling. On either side, the hall opened out into long corridors, while straight ahead a massive stairway swept majestically toward the upper floors.

For a moment T'sinadree hesitated. Then, since one

way was as good as another, he led his companions down the first corridor.

The feeling that life was near had now become very strong. At any moment, it seemed, they might be confronted by the creatures of this world. If they showed hostility—and they could scarcely be blamed if they did—the paralyzers would be used at once.

The tension was very great as the party entered the first room, and only relaxed when they saw that it held nothing but machines—row after row of them, now stilled and silent. Lining the enormous room were thousands of metal filing cabinets, forming a continuous wall as far as the eye could reach. And that was all; there was no furniture, nothing but the cabinets and the mysterious machines.

Alarkane, always the quickest of the three, was already examining the cabinets. Each held many thousand sheets of tough, thin material, perforated with innumerable holes and slots. The Paladorian appropriated one of the cards and Alarkane recorded the scene together with some close-ups of the machines. Then they left. The great room, which had been one of the marvels of the world, meant nothing to them. No living eye would ever again see that wonderful battery of almost human Hollerith analyzers and the five thousand million punched cards holding all that could be recorded of each man, woman and child on the planet.

It was clear that this building had been used very recently. With growing excitement, the explorers hurried on to the next room. This they found to be an enormous library, for millions of books lay all around them on miles and miles of shelving. Here, though the explorers could not know it, were the records of all the laws that Man had ever passed, and all the speeches that had ever been made in his council chambers.

T'sinadree was deciding his plan of action, when Alarkane drew his attention to one of the racks a hundred yards away. It was half empty, unlike all the others. Around it books lay in a tumbled heap on the floor, as if knocked down by someone in frantic haste. The signs were unmistakable. Not long ago, other creatures had been this way. Faint wheel marks were clearly visible on the floor to the acute sense of Alarkane, though the others could see nothing. Alarkane could even detect footprints, but knowing nothing of the creatures that had formed them he could not say which way they led.

The sense of nearness was stronger than ever now, but it was nearness in time, not in space. Alarkane voiced the thoughts of the party.

"Those books must have been valuable, and someone has come to rescue them—rather as an afterthought, I should say. That means there must be a place of refuge, possibly not very far away. Perhaps we may be able to find some other clues that will lead us to it."

T'sinadree agreed; the Paladorian wasn't enthusiastic.

"That may be so," it said, "but the refuge may be anywhere on the planet, and we have just two hours left. Let us waste no more time if we hope to rescue these people."

The party hurried forward once more, pausing only to collect a few books that might be useful to the scientists at Base—though it was doubtful if they could ever be translated. They soon found that the great building was composed largely of small rooms, all showing signs of recent occupation. Most of them were in a neat and tidy condition, but one or two were very much the reverse. The explorers were particularly puzzled by one room—clearly an office of some kind—that appeared to have been completely wrecked. The floor was littered with papers, the furniture had been smashed, and smoke was pouring through the broken windows from the fires outside.

T'sinadree was rather alarmed.

"Surely no dangerous animal could have got into a place like this!" he exclaimed, fingering his paralyzer nervously.

Alarkane did not answer. He began to make that annoying sound which his race called "laughter." It was several minutes before he would explain what had amused him.

"I don't think any animal has done it," he said. "In fact, the explanation is very simple. Suppose *you* had been working all your life in this room, dealing with endless papers, year after year. And suddenly, you are told that you will never see it again, that your work is finished, and that you can leave it forever. More than that—no one will come after you. Everything is finished. How would you make your exit, T'sinadree?"

The other thought for a moment.

"Well, I suppose I'd just tidy things up and leave. That's what seems to have happened in all the other rooms."

Alarkane laughed again.

"I'm quite sure you would. But some individuals have a different psychology. I think I should have liked the creature that used this room."

He did not explain himself further, and his two colleagues puzzled over his words for quite a while before they gave it up.

It came as something of a shock when Torkalee gave the order to return. They had gathered a great deal of information, but had found no clue that might lead them to the missing inhabitants of this world. That problem was as baffling as ever, and now it seemed that it would never be solved. There were only forty minutes left before the S9000 would be departing.

They were halfway back to the tender when they saw the semicircular passage leading down into the depths of the building. Its architectural style was quite different from that used elsewhere, and the gently sloping floor was an irresistible attraction to creatures whose many legs had grown weary of the marble staircases which only bipeds could have built in such profusion. T'sinadree had been the worst sufferer, for he normally employed twelve legs and could use twenty when he was in a hurry, though no one had ever seen him perform this feat.

The party stopped dead and looked down the passageway with a single thought. A tunnel, leading down into the depths of Earth! At its end, they might yet find the people of this world and rescue some of them from their fate. For there was still time to call the mother ship if the need arose.

T'sinadree signaled to his commander and Torkalee brought the little machine immediately overhead. There might not be time for the party to retrace its footsteps through the maze of passages, so meticulously recorded in the Paladorian mind that there was no possibility of going astray. If speed was necessary, Torkalee could blast his way through the dozen floors above their head. In any case, it should not take long to find what lay at the end of the passage.

It took only thirty seconds. The tunnel ended quite abruptly in a very curious cylindrical room with magnificently padded seats along the walls. There was no way out save that by which they had come and it was several seconds before the purpose of the chamber dawned on Alarkane's mind. It was a pity, he thought, that they would never have time to use this. The thought was suddenly interrupted by a cry from T'sinadree. Alarkane wheeled around, and saw that the entrance had closed silently behind them.

Even in that first moment of panic, Alarkane found himself thinking with some admiration: Whoever they were, they knew how to build automatic machinery!

The Paladorian was the first to speak. It waved one of its tentacles toward the seats.

"We think it would be best to be seated," it said. The multiplex mind of Palador had already analyzed the situation and knew what was coming.

They did not have long to wait before a low-pitched hum came from a grill overhead, and for the very last time in history a human, even if lifeless, voice was heard on Earth. The words were meaningless, though the trapped explorers could guess their message clearly enough.

"Choose your stations, please, and be seated."

Simultaneously, a wall panel at one end of the compartment glowed with light. On it was a simple map, consisting of a series of a dozen circles connected by a line. Each of the circles had writing alongside it, and beside the writing were two buttons of different colors.

Alarkane looked questioningly at his leader.

"Don't touch them," said T'sinadree. "If we leave the controls alone, the doors may open again."

He was wrong. The engineers who had designed the automatic subway had assumed that anyone who entered it would naturally wish to go somewhere. If they selected no intermediate station, their destination could only be the end of the line.

There was another pause while the relays and thyratrons waited for their orders. In those thirty seconds, if they had known what to do, the party could have opened the doors and left the subway. But they did not know, and the machines geared to a human psychology acted for them.

The surge of acceleration was not very great; the lavish upholstery was a luxury, not a necessity. Only an almost imperceptible vibration told of the speed at which they were traveling through the bowels of the earth, on a journey the duration of which they could not even guess. And in thirty minutes, the S9000 would be leaving the Solar System.

There was a long silence in the speeding machine. T'sinadree and Alarkane were thinking rapidly. So was the Paladorian, though in a different fashion. The conception of personal death was meaningless to it, for the destruction of a single unit meant no more to the group mind than the loss of a nail-paring to a man. But it could, though with great difficulty, appreciate the plight of individual intelligences such as Alarkane and T'sinadree, and it was anxious to help them if it could.

Alarkane had managed to contact Torkalee with his personal transmitter, though the signal was very weak and seemed to be fading quickly. Rapidly he explained the situation, and almost at once the signals became clearer. Torkalee was following the path of the machine, flying above the ground under which they were speeding to their unknown destination. That was the first indication they had of the fact that they were traveling at nearly a thousand miles an hour, and very soon after that Torkalee was able to give the still more disturbing news that they were rapidly approaching the sea. While they were beneath the land, there was a hope, though a slender one, that they might stop the machine and escape. But under the ocean—not all the brains and the machinery in the great mother ship could save them. No one could have devised a more perfect trap.

T'sinadree had been examining the wall map with great attention. Its meaning was obvious, and along the line connecting the circles a tiny spot of light was crawling. It was already halfway to the first of the stations marked.

"I'm going to press one of those buttons," said T'sinadree at last. "It won't do any harm, and we may learn something."

"I agree. Which will you try first?"

"There are only two kinds, and it won't matter if we try the wrong one first. I suppose one is to start the machine and the other is to stop it."

Alarkane was not very hopeful.

"It started without any button pressing," he said. "I think it's completely automatic and we can't control it from here at all."

T'sinadree could not agree.

"These buttons are clearly associated with the stations, and there's no point in having them unless you can use them to stop yourself. The only question is, which is the right one?"

His analysis was perfectly correct. The machine could be stopped at any intermediate station. They had only been on their way ten minutes, and if they could leave now, no harm would have been done. It was just bad luck that T'sinadree's first choice was the wrong button.

The little light on the map crawled slowly through the illuminated circle without checking its speed. And at the same time Torkalee called from the ship overhead.

"You have just passed underneath a city and are heading out to sea. There cannot be another stop for nearly a thousand miles."

Alveron had given up all hope of finding life on this world. The S9000 had roamed over half the planet, never staying long in one place, descending ever and again in an effort to attract attention. There had been no response; Earth seemed utterly dead. If any of its inhabitants were still alive, thought Alveron, they must have hidden themselves in its depths where no help could reach them, though their doom would be nonetheless certain.

Rugon brought news of the disaster. The great ship ceased its fruitless searching and fled back through the storm to the ocean above which Torkalee's little tender was still following the track of the buried machine.

The scene was truly terrifying. Not since the days when Earth was born had there been such seas as this. Mountains of water were racing before the storm which had now reached velocities of many hundred miles an hour. Even at this distance from the mainland the air was full of flying debris—trees, fragments of houses, sheets of metal, anything that had not been anchored to the ground. No airborne machine could have lived for a moment in such a gale. And ever and again even the roar of the wind was drowned as the vast water-mountains met head-on with a crash that seemed to shake the sky.

Fortunately, there had been no serious earthquakes yet. Far beneath the bed of the ocean, the wonderful piece of engineering which had been the World President's private vacuum-subway was still working perfectly, unaffected by the tumult and destruction above. It would continue to work until the last minute of the Earth's existence, which, if the astronomers were right, was not much more than fifteen minutes away—though precisely how much more Alveron would have given a great deal to know. It would be nearly an hour before the trapped party could reach land and even the slightest hope of rescue.

Alveron's instructions had been precise, though even without them he would never have dreamed of taking any risks with the great machine that had been entrusted to his care. Had he been human, the decision to abandon the trapped members of his crew would have been desperately hard to make. But he came of a race far more sensitive than Man, a race that so loved the things of the spirit that long ago, and with infinite reluctance, it had taken over control of the Universe since only thus could it be sure that justice was being done. Alveron would need all his superhuman gifts to carry him through the next few hours.

Meanwhile, a mile below the bed of the ocean Alarkane

and T'sinadree were very busy indeed with their private communicators. Fifteen minutes is not a long time in which to wind up the affairs of a lifetime. It is indeed, scarcely long enough to dictate more than a few of those farewell messages which at such moments are so much more important than all other matters.

All the while the Paladorian had remained silent and motionless, saying not a word. The other two, resigned to their fate and engrossed in their personal affairs, had given it no thought. They were startled when suddenly it began to address them in its peculiarly passionless voice.

"We perceive that you are making certain arrangements concerning your anticipated destruction. That will probably be unnecessary. Captain Alveron hopes to rescue us if we can stop this machine when we reach land again."

Both T'sinadree and Alarkane were too surprised to say anything for a moment. Then the latter gasped, "How do you know?"

It was a foolish question, for he remembered at once that there were several Paladorians—if one could use the phrase—in the S9000, and consequently their companion knew everything that was happening in the mother ship. So he did not wait for an answer but continued, "Alveron can't do that! He daren't take such a risk!"

"There will be no risk," said the Paladorian. "We have told him what to do. It is really very simple."

Alarkane and T'sinadree looked at their companion with something approaching awe, realizing now what must have happened. In moments of crisis, the single units comprising the Paladorian mind could link together in an organization no less close than that of any physical brain. At such moments they formed an intellect more powerful than any other in the Universe. All ordinary problems could be solved by a few hundred or thousand units. Very rarely, millions would be needed, and on two historic occasions the billions of cells of the entire Paladorian consciousness had been welded together to deal with emergencies that threatened the race. The mind of Palador was one of the greatest mental resources of the Universe; its full force was seldom required, but the knowledge that it was available was supremely comforting to other races. Alarkane wondered how many cells had co-ordinated to deal with this particular emergency. He also wondered how so trivial an incident had ever come to its attention.

To that question he was never to know the answer, though he might have guessed it had he known that the chillingly remote Paladorian mind possessed an almost human streak of vanity. Long ago, Alarkane had written a book trying to prove that eventually all intelligent races would sacrifice individual consciousness and that one day only group-minds would remain in the Universe. Palador, he had said, was the first of those ultimate intellects, and the vast, dispersed mind had not been displeased.

They had no time to ask any further questions before Alveron himself began to speak through their communicators.

"Alveron calling! We're staying on this planet until the detonation waves reach it, so we may be able to rescue you. You're heading toward a city on the coast which you'll reach in forty minutes at your present speed. If you cannot stop yourselves then, we're going to blast the tunnel behind and ahead of you to cut off your power. Then we'll sink a shaft to get you out—the chief engineer says he can do it in five minutes with the main projectors. So you should be safe within an hour, unless the sun blows up before."

"And if that happens, you'll be destroyed as well! You mustn't take such a risk!"

"Don't let that worry you; we're perfectly safe. When the sun detonates, the explosion wave will take several minutes to rise to its maximum. But apart from that, we're on the night side of the planet, behind an eight-thousand-mile screen of rock. When the first warning of the explosion comes, we will accelerate out of the Solar System, keeping in the shadow of the planet. Under our maximum drive, we will reach the velocity of light before leaving the cone of shadow, and the sun cannot harm us then."

T'sinadree was still afraid to hope. Another objection came at once into his mind.

"Yes, but how will you get any warning, here on the night side of the planet?"

"Very easily," replied Alveron. "This world has a moon which is now visible from this hemisphere. We have telescopes trained on it. If it shows any sudden increase in brilliance, our main drive goes on automatically and we'll be thrown out of the system."

The logic was flawless. Alveron, cautious as ever, was taking no chances. It would be many minutes before the eight-thousand-mile shield of rock and metal could be destroyed by the fires of the exploding sun. In that time, the S9000 could have reached the safety of the velocity of light.

Alarkane pressed the second button when they were still several miles from the coast. He did not expect anything to happen then, assuming that the machine could not stop between stations. It seemed too good to be true when, a few minutes later, the machine's slight vibration died away and they came to a halt.

The doors slid silently apart. Even before they were fully open, the three had left the compartment. They were taking no more chances. Before them a long tunnel stretched into the distance, rising slowly out of sight. They were starting along it when suddenly Alveron's voice called from the communicators.

"Stay where you are! We're going to blast!"

The ground shuddered once, and far ahead there came the rumble of falling rock. Again the earth shook—and a hundred yards ahead the passageway vanished abruptly. A tremendous vertical shaft had been cut clean through it.

The party hurried forward again until they came to the end of the corridor and stood waiting on its lip. The shaft in which it ended was a full thousand feet across and descended into the earth as far as the torches could throw their beams. Overhead, the storm clouds fled beneath a moon that no man would have recognized, so luridly brilliant was its disk. And, most glorious of all sights, the S9000 floated high above, the great projectors that had drilled this enormous pit still glowing cherry red.

A dark shape detached itself from the mother ship and

dropped swiftly toward the ground. Torkalee was returning to collect his friends. A little later, Alveron greeted them in the control room. He waved to the great vision screen and said quietly, "See, we were barely in time."

The continent below them was slowly settling beneath the mile-high waves that were attacking its coasts. The last that anyone was ever to see of Earth was a great plain, bathed with the silver light of the abnormally brilliant moon. Across its face the waters were pouring in a glittering flood toward a distant range of mountains. The sea had won its final victory, but its triumph would be short-lived for soon sea and land would be no more. Even as the silent party in the control room watched the destruction below, the infinitely greater catastrophe to which this was only the prelude came swiftly upon them.

It was as though dawn had broken suddenly over this moonlit landscape. But it was not dawn: it was only the moon, shining with the brilliance of a second sun. For perhaps thirty seconds that awesome, unnatural light burnt fiercely on the doomed land beneath. Then there came a sudden flashing of indicator lights across the control board. The main drive was on. For a second Alveron glanced at the indicators and checked their information. When he looked again at the screen, Earth was gone.

The magnificent, desperately overstrained generators quietly died when the S9000 was passing the orbit of Persephone. It did not matter, the sun could never harm them now, and although the ship was speeding helplessly out into the lonely night of interstellar space, it would only be a matter of days before rescue came.

There was irony in that. A day ago, they had been the rescuers, going to the aid of a race that now no longer existed. Not for the first time Alveron wondered about the world that had just perished. He tried, in vain, to picture it as it had been in its glory, the streets of its cities thronged with life. Primitive though its people had been, they might have offered much to the Universe. If only they could have made contact! Regret was useless; long before their coming, the people of this world must have buried themselves in its iron heart. And now they and their civilization would remain a mystery for the rest of time.

Alveron was glad when his thoughts were interrupted by Rugon's entrance. The chief of communications had been very busy ever since the take-off, trying to analyze the programs radiated by the transmitter Orostron had discovered. The problem was not a difficult one, but it demanded the construction of special equipment, and that had taken time.

"Well, what have you found?" asked Alveron.

"Quite a lot," replied his friend. "There's something mysterious here, and I don't understand it.

"It didn't take long to find how the vision transmissions were built up, and we've been able to convert them to suit our own equipment. It seems that there were cameras all over the planet, surveying points of interest. Some of them were apparently in cities, on the tops of very high buildings. The cameras were rotating continuously to give panoramic views. In the programs we've recorded there are about twenty different scenes.

"In addition, there are a number of transmissions of a different kind, neither sound nor vision. They seem to be purely scientific—possibly instrument readings or something of that sort. All these programs were going out simultaneously on different frequency bands.

"Now there must be a reason for all this. Orostron still thinks that the station simply wasn't switched off when it was deserted. But these aren't the sort of programs such a station would normally radiate at all. It was certainly used for interplanetary relaying—Klarten was quite right there. So these people must have crossed space, since none of the other planets had any life at the time of the last survey. Don't you agree?"

Alveron was following intently.

"Yes, that seems reasonable enough. But it's also certain that the beam was pointing to none of the other planets. I checked that myself."

"I know," said Rugon. "What I want to discover is why a giant interplanetary relay station is busily transmitting pictures of a world about to be destroyed—pictures that would be of immense interest to scientists and astrono-mers. Someone had gone to a lot of trouble to arrange all those panoramic cameras. I am convinced that those beams were going somewhere."

Alveron started up.

"Do you imagine that there might be an outer planet that hasn't been reported?" he asked. "If so, your theory's certainly wrong. The beam wasn't even pointing in the plane of the Solar System. And even if it were—just look at this."

He switched on the vision screen and adjusted the con-trols. Against the velvet curtain of space was hanging a blue-white sphere, apparently composed of many concen-tric shells of incandescent gas. Even though its immense distance made all movement invisible, it was clearly ex-panding at an enormous rate. At its center was a blinding point of light—the white dwarf star that the sun had now become.

"You probably don't realize just how big that sphere is," said Alveron. "Look at this."

He increased the magnification until only the center portion of the nova was visible. Close to its heart were two minute condensations, one on either side of the nucleus.

"Those are the two giant planets of the system. They have still managed to retain their existence—after a fashion. And they were several hundred million miles from the sun. The nova is still expanding—but it's already twice the size of the Solar System."

Rugon was silent for a moment.

"Perhaps you're right," he said, rather grudgingly. "You've disposed of my first theory. But you still haven't satisfied me."

He made several swift circuits of the room before speaking again. Alveron waited patiently. He knew the almost intuitive powers of his friend, who could often solve a problem when mere logic seemed insufficient.

Then, rather slowly, Rugon began to speak again.

"What do you think of this?" he said. "Suppose we've completely underestimated this people? Orostron did it once—he thought they could never have crossed space, since they'd only known radio for two centuries. Hansur II told me that. Well, Orostron was quite wrong. Perhaps we're all wrong. I've had a look at the material that Klarten brought back from the transmitter. He wasn't impressed by what he found, but it's a marvelous achievement for so short a time. There were devices in that station that belonged to civilizations thousands of years older. Alveron, can we follow that beam to see where it leads?"

Alveron said nothing for a full minute. He had been more than half expecting the question, but it was not an easy one to answer. The main generators had gone completely. There was no point in trying to repair them. But there was still power available, and while there was power, anything could be done in time. It would mean a lot of improvisation, and some difficult maneuvers, for the ship still had its enormous initial velocity. Yes, it could be done, and the activity would keep the crew from becoming further depressed, now that the reaction caused by the mission's failure had started to set in. The news that the nearest heavy repair ship could not reach them for three weeks had also caused a slump in morale.

The engineers, as usual, made a tremendous fuss. Again as usual, they did the job in half the time they had dismissed as being absolutely impossible. Very slowly, over many hours, the great ship began to discard the speed its main drive had given it in as many minutes. In a tremendous curve, millions of miles in radius, the S9000 changed its course and the star fields shifted round it.

The maneuver took three days, but at the end of that time the ship was limping along a course parallel to the beam that had once come from Earth. They were heading out into emptiness, the blazing sphere that had been the sun dwindling slowly behind them. By the standards of interstellar flight, they were almost stationary.

For hours Rugon strained over his instruments, driving his detector beams far ahead into space. There were certainly no planets within many light-years; there was no doubt of that. From time to time Alveron came to see him and always he had to give the same reply: "Nothing to report." About a fifth of the time Rugon's intuition let him down badly; he began to wonder if this was such an occasion.

Not until a week later did the needles of the mass-detectors quiver feebly at the ends of their scales. But Rugon said nothing, not even to his captain. He waited until he was sure, and he went on waiting until even the short-range scanners began to react, and to build up the first faint pictures on the vision screen. Still he waited patiently until he could interpret the images. Then, when he knew that his wildest fancy was even less than the truth, he called his colleagues into the control room.

The picture on the vision screen was the familiar one of endless star fields, sun beyond sun to the very limits of the Universe. Near the center of the screen a distant nebula made a patch of haze that was difficult for the eye to grasp.

Rugon increased the magnification. The stars flowed out of the field; the little nebula expanded until it filled the screen and then—it was a nebula no longer. A simultaneous gasp of amazement came from all the company at the sight that lay before them.

Lying across league after league of space, ranged in a vast three-dimensional array of rows and columns with the precision of a marching army, were thousands of tiny pencils of light. They were moving swiftly; the whole immense lattice holding its shape as a single unit. Even as Alveron and his comrades watched, the formation began to drift off the screen and Rugon had to recenter the controls.

After a long pause, Rugon started to speak.

"This is the race," he said softly, "that has known radio for only two centuries—the race that we believed had crept to die in the heart of its planet. I have examined those images under the highest possible magnification.

"That is the greatest fleet of which there has ever been a record. Each of those points of light represents a ship larger than our own. Of course, they are very primitive—what you see on the screen are the jets of their rockets. Yes, they dared to use rockets to bridge interstellar space!

You realize what that means. It would take them centuries to reach the nearest star. The whole race must have embarked on this journey in the hope that its descendants would complete it, generations later.

"To measure the extent of their accomplishment, think of the ages it took us to conquer space, and the longer ages still before we attempted to reach the stars. Even if we were threatened with annihilation, could we have done so much in so short a time? Remember, this is the youngest civilization in the Universe. Four hundred thousand years ago it did not even exist. What will it be a million years from now?"

An hour later, Orostron left the crippled mother ship to make contact with the great fleet ahead. As the little torpedo disappeared among the stars, Alveron turned to his friend and made a remark that Rugon was often to remember in the years ahead.

"I wonder what they'll be like?" he mused. "Will they be nothing but wonderful engineers, with no art or philosophy? They're going to have such a surprise when Orostron reaches them—I expect it will be rather a blow to their pride. It's funny how all isolated races think they're the only people in the Universe. But they should be grateful to us; we're going to save them a good many hundred years of travel."

Alveron glanced at the Milky Way, lying like a veil of silver mist across the vision screen. He waved toward it with a sweep of a tentacle that embraced the whole circle of the galaxy, from the Central Planets to the lonely suns of the Rim.

"You know," he said to Rugon, "I feel rather afraid of these people. Suppose they don't like our little Federation?" He waved once more toward the star-clouds that lay massed across the screen, glowing with the light of their countless suns.

"Something tells me they'll be very determined people," he added. "We had better be polite to them. After all, we only outnumber them about a thousand million to one."

Rugon laughed at his captain's little joke.

Twenty years afterward, the remark didn't seem funny.

A Walk in the Dark

ROBERT ARMSTRONG HAD WALKED JUST OVER TWO MILES, AS far as he could judge, when his torch failed. He stood still for a moment, unable to believe that such a misfortune could really have befallen him. Then, half maddened with rage, he hurled the useless instrument away. It landed somewhere in the darkness, disturbing the silence of this little world. A metallic echo came ringing back from the low hills: then all was quiet again.

This, thought Armstrong, was the ultimate misfortune. Nothing more could happen to him now. He was even able to laugh bitterly at his luck, and resolved never again to imagine that the fickle goddess had ever favored him. Who would have believed that the only tractor at Camp IV would have broken down when he was just setting off for Port Sanderson? He recalled the frenzied repair work, the relief when the second start had been made—and the final debacle when the caterpillar track had jammed.

It was no use then regretting the lateness of his departure: he could not have foreseen these accidents, and it was still a good four hours before the "Canopus" took off. He *had* to catch her, whatever happened; no other ship would be touching at this world for another month.

Apart from the urgency of his business, four more weeks on this out-of-the-way planet were unthinkable.

There had been only one thing to do. It was lucky that Port Sanderson was little more than six miles from the camp—not a great distance, even on foot. He had had to leave all his equipment behind, but it could follow on the next ship and he could manage without it. The road was poor, merely stamped out of the rock by one of the Board's hundred-ton crushers, but there was no fear of going astray.

Even now, he was in no real danger, though he might well be too late to catch the ship. Progress would be slow, for he dare not risk losing the road in this region of canyons and enigmatic tunnels that had never been explored. It was, of course, pitch-dark. Here at the edge of the galaxy the stars were so few and scattered that their light was negligible. The strange crimson sun of this lonely world would not rise for many hours, and although five of the little moons were in the sky they could barely be seen by the unaided eye. Not one of them could even cast a shadow.

Armstrong was not the man to bewail his luck for long. He began to walk slowly along the road, feeling its texture with his feet. It was, he knew, fairly straight except where it wound through Carver's Pass. He wished he had a stick or something to probe the way before him, but he would have to rely for guidance on the feel of the ground.

It was terribly slow at first, until he gained confidence. He had never known how difficult it was to walk in a straight line. Although the feeble stars gave him his bearings, again and again he found himself stumbling among the virgin rocks at the edge of the crude roadway. He was traveling in long zigzags that took him to alternate sides of the road. Then he would stub his toes against the bare rock and grope his way back on to the hard-packed surface once again.

Presently it settled down to a routine. It was impossible to estimate his speed; he could only struggle along and hope for the best. There were four miles to go—four miles and as many hours. It should be easy enough, unless he lost his way. But he dared not think of that.

Once he had mastered the technique he could afford the luxury of thought. He could not pretend that he was enjoying the experience, but he had been in much worse positions before. As long as he remained on the road, he was perfectly safe. He had been hoping that as his eyes became adapted to the starlight he would be able to see the way, but he now knew that the whole journey would be blind. The discovery gave him a vivid sense of his remoteness from the heart of the Galaxy. On a night as clear as this, the skies of almost any other planet would have been blazing with stars. Here at this outpost of the Universe the sky held perhaps a hundred faintly gleaming points of light, as useless as the five ridiculous moons on which no one had ever bothered to land.

A slight change in the road interrupted his thoughts. Was there a curve here, or had he veered off to the right again? He moved very slowly along the invisible and ill-defined border. Yes, there was no mistake: the road was bending to the left. He tried to remember its appearance in the daytime, but he had only seen it once before. Did this mean that he was nearing the Pass? He hoped so, for the journey would then be half completed.

He peered ahead into the blackness, but the ragged line of the horizon told him nothing. Presently he found that the road had straightened itself again and his spirits sank. The entrance to the Pass must still be some way ahead: there were at least four miles to go.

Four miles—how ridiculous the distance seemed! How long would it take the "Canopus" to travel four miles? He doubted if man could measure so short an interval of time. And how many trillions of miles had he, Robert Armstrong, traveled in his life? It must have reached a staggering total by now, for in the last twenty years he had scarcely stayed more than a month at a time on any single world. This very year, he had twice made the crossing of the Galaxy, and that was a notable journey even in these days of the phantom drive.

He tripped over a loose stone, and the jolt brought him back to reality. It was no use, here, thinking of ships that could eat up the light-years. He was facing nature, with no weapons but his own strength and skill.

It was strange that it took him so long to identify the real cause of his uneasiness. The last four weeks had been very full, and the rush of his departure, coupled with the annoyance and anxiety caused by the tractor's break-downs, had driven everything else from his mind. More-over, he had always prided himself on his hard-headed-ness and lack of imagination. Until now, he had forgotten all about that first evening at the Base, when the crews had regaled him with the usual tall yarns concocted for the benefit of newcomers.

It was then that the old Base clerk had told the story of his walk by night from Port Sanderson to the camp, and of what had trailed him through Carver's Pass, keeping always beyond the limit of his torchlight. Armstrong, who had heard such tales on a score of worlds, had paid it little attention at the time. This planet, after all, was known to be uninhabited. But logic could not dispose of the matter as easily as that. Suppose, after all, there was some truth in the old man's fantastic tale . . . ?

It was not a pleasant thought, and Armstrong did not intend to brood upon it. But he knew that if he dismissed it out of hand it would continue to prey on his mind. The only way to conquer imaginary fears was to face them boldly; he would have to do that now.

His strongest argument was the complete barrenness of this world and its utter desolation, though against that one could set many counter-arguments, as indeed the old clerk had done. Man had only lived on this planet for twenty years, and much of it was still unexplored. No one could deny that the tunnels out in the wasteland were rather puzzling, but everyone believed them to be volcanic vents. Though, of course, life often crept into such places. With a shudder he remembered the giant polyps that had snared the first explorers of Vargon III.

It was all very inconclusive. Suppose, for the sake of argument, one granted the existence of life here. What of that?

The vast majority of life forms in the Universe were completely indifferent to man. Some, of course, like the gas-beings of Alcoran or the roving wave-lattices of Shandaloon, could not even detect him but passed through or around him as if he did not exist. Others were merely inquisitive, some embarrassingly friendly. There were few indeed that would attack unless provoked.

Nevertheless, it was a grim picture that the old stores clerk had painted. Back in the warm, well-lighted smoking-room, with the drinks going around, it had been easy enough to laugh at it. But here in the darkness, miles from any human settlement, it was very different.

It was almost a relief when he stumbled off the road again and had to grope with his hands until he found it once more. This seemed a very rough patch, and the road was scarcely distinguishable from the rocks around. In a few minutes, however, he was safely on his way again.

It was unpleasant to see how quickly his thoughts returned to the same disquieting subject. Clearly it was worrying him more than he cared to admit.

He drew consolation from one fact: it had been quite obvious that no one at the base had believed the old fellow's story. Their questions and banter had proved that. At the time, he had laughed as loudly as any of them. After all, what *was* the evidence? A dim shape, just seen in the darkness, that might well have been an oddly formed rock. And the curious clicking noise that had so impressed the old man—anyone could imagine such sounds at night if they were sufficiently overwrought. If it had been hostile, why hadn't the creature come any closer? "Because it was afraid of my light," the old chap had said. Well, that was plausible enough: it would explain why nothing had ever been seen in the daylight. Such a creature might live underground, only emerging at night—damn it, why was he taking the old idiot's ravings so seriously! Armstrong got control of his thoughts again. If he went on this way, he told himself angrily, he would soon be seeing and hearing a whole menagerie of monsters.

There was, of course, one factor that disposed of the ridiculous story at once. It was really very simple; he felt sorry he hadn't thought of it before. *What would such a creature live on?* There was not even a trace of vegetation on the whole of the planet. He laughed to think that the bogy could be disposed of so easily—and in the same instant felt annoyed with himself for not laughing aloud. If he was so sure of his reasoning, why not whistle, or sing, or do anything to keep up his spirits? He put the question fairly to himself as a test of his manhood. Half-ashamed, he had to admit that he was still afraid—

afraid because "there *might* be something in it, after all."
But at least his analysis had done him some good.

It would have been better if he had left it there, and
remained half-convinced by his argument. But a part of
his mind was still busily trying to break down his careful
reasoning. It succeeded only too well, and when he remembered the plant-beings of Xantil Major the shock was
so unpleasant that he stopped dead in his tracks.

Now the plant-beings of Xantil were not in any way
horrible. They were in fact extremely beautiful creatures.
But what made them appear so distressing now was the
knowledge that they could live for indefinite periods with
no food whatsoever. All the energy they needed for their
strange lives they extracted from cosmic radiation—and
that was almost as intense here as anywhere else in the
universe.

He had scarcely thought of one example before others
crowded into his mind and he remembered the life form
on Trantor Beta, which was the only one known capable
of directly utilizing atomic energy. That too had lived
on an utterly barren world, very much like this . . .

Armstrong's mind was rapidly splitting into two distinct portions, each trying to convince the other and
neither wholly succeeding. He did not realize how far his
morale had gone until he found himself holding his breath
lest it conceal any sound from the darkness about him.
Angrily, he cleared his mind of the rubbish that had been
gathering there and turned once more to the immediate
problem.

There was no doubt that the road was slowly rising,
and the silhouette of the horizon seemed much higher in
the sky. The road began to twist, and suddenly he was
aware of great rocks on either side of him. Soon only a
narrow ribbon of sky was still visible, and the darkness
became, if possible, even more intense.

Somehow, he felt safer with the rock walls surrounding
him: it meant that he was protected except in two directions. Also, the road had been levelled more carefully and
it was easy to keep it. Best of all, he knew now that the
journey was more than half completed.

For a moment his spirits began to rise. Then, with maddening perversity, his mind went back into the old grooves again. He remembered that it was on the far side of Carver's Pass that the old clerk's adventure had taken place—if it had ever happened at all.

In half a mile, he would be out in the open again, out of the protection of these sheltering rocks. The thought seemed doubly horrible now and he already felt a sense of nakedness. He could be attacked from any direction, and he would be utterly helpless . . .

Until now, he had still retained some self-control. Very resolutely he had kept his mind away from the one fact that gave some color to the old man's tale—the single piece of evidence that had stopped the banter in the crowded room back at the camp and brought a sudden hush upon the company. Now, as Armstrong's will weakened, he recalled again the words that had struck a momentary chill even in the warm comfort of the base building.

The little clerk had been very insistent on one point. He had never heard any sound of pursuit from the dim shape sensed, rather than seen, at the limit of his light. There was no scuffling of claws or hoofs on rock, nor even the clatter of displaced stones. It was as if, so the old man had declared in that solemn manner of his, "as if the thing that was following could see perfectly in the darkness, and had many small legs or pads so that it could move swiftly and easily over the rock—like a giant caterpillar or one of the carpet-things of Kralkor II."

Yet, although there had been no noise of pursuit, there had been one sound that the old man had caught several times. It was so unusual that its very strangeness made it doubly ominous. It was a faint but horribly persistent *clicking*.

The old fellow had been able to describe it very vividly —much too vividly for Armstrong's liking now.

"Have you ever listened to a large insect crunching its prey?" he said. "Well, it was just like that. I imagine that a crab makes exactly the same noise with its claws when it clashes them together. It was a—what's the word?—a *chitinous* sound."

At this point, Armstrong remembered laughing loudly. (Strange, how it was all coming back to him now.) But no one else had laughed, though they had been quick to do so earlier. Sensing the change of tone, he had sobered at once and asked the old man to continue his story. How he wished now that he had stifled his curiosity!

It had been quickly told. The next day, a party of skeptical technicians had gone into the no-man's land beyond Carver's Pass. They were not skeptical enough to leave their guns behind, but they had no cause to use them for they found no trace of any living thing. There were the inevitable pits and tunnels, glistening holes down which the light of the torches rebounded endlessly until it was lost in the distance—but the planet was riddled with them.

Though the party found no sign of life, it discovered one thing it did not like at all. Out in the barren and unexplored land beyond the Pass they had come upon an even larger tunnel than the rest. Near the mouth of that tunnel was a massive rock, half embedded in the ground. And the sides of that rock had been worn away *as if it had been used as an enormous whetstone.*

No less than five of those present had seen this disturbing rock. None of them could explain it satisfactorily as a natural formation, but they still refused to accept the old man's story. Armstrong had asked them if they had ever put it to the test. There had been an uncomfortable silence. Then big Andrew Hargraves had said: "Hell, who'd walk out to the Pass at night just for fun!" and had left it at that. Indeed, there was no other record of anyone walking from Port Sanderson to the camp by night, or for that matter by day. During the hours of light, no unprotected human being could live in the open beneath the rays of the enormous, lurid sun that seemed to fill half the sky. And no one would walk six miles, wearing radiation armor, if the tractor was available.

Armstrong felt that he was leaving the Pass. The rocks on either side were falling away, and the road was no longer as firm and well packed as it had been. He was coming out into the open plain once more, and somewhere not far away in the darkness was that enigmatic pillar that might have been used for sharpening monstrous fangs or claws. It was not a reassuring thought, but he could not get it out of his mind.

Feeling distinctly worried now, Armstrong made a great effort to pull himself together. He would try to be rational again; he would think of business, the work he had done at the camp—anything but this infernal place. For a while, he succeeded quite well. But presently, with a maddening persistence, every train of thought came back to the same point. He could not get out of his mind the picture of that inexplicable rock and its appalling possibilities. Over and over again he found himself wondering how far away it was, whether he had already passed it, and whether it was on his right or his left. . . .

The ground was quite flat again, and the road drove on straight as an arrow. There was one gleam of consolation: Port Sanderson could not be much more than two miles away. Armstrong had no idea how long he had been on the road. Unfortunately his watch was not illuminated and he could only guess at the passage of time. With any luck, the "Canopus" should not take off for another two hours at least. But he could not be sure, and now another fear began to enter his mind—the dread that he might see a vast constellation of lights rising swiftly into the sky ahead, and know that all this agony of mind had been in vain.

He was not zigzagging so badly now, and seemed to be able to anticipate the edge of the road before stumbling off it. It was probable, he cheered himself by thinking, that he was traveling almost as fast as if he had a light. If all went well, he might be nearing Port Sanderson in thirty minutes—a ridiculously small space of time. How he would laugh at his fears when he strolled into his already reserved stateroom in the "Canopus," and felt that peculiar quiver as the phantom drive hurled the great ship far out of this system, back to the clustered star-clouds near the center of the Galaxy—back toward Earth itself, which he had not seen for so many years. One day, he told himself, he really must visit Earth again. All his life he had been making the promise, but always there had been the same answer—lack of time. Strange, wasn't it, that such a tiny planet should have played so enormous a part in the development of the Universe, should even have come to dominate worlds far wiser and more intelligent than itself!

Armstrong's thoughts were harmless again, and he felt calmer. The knowledge that he was nearing Port Sanderson was immensely reassuring, and he deliberately kept his mind on familiar, unimportant matters. Carver's Pass was already far behind, and with it that thing he no longer intended to recall. One day, if he ever returned to this world, he would visit the pass in the daytime and laugh at his fears. In twenty minutes now, they would have joined the nightmares of his childhood.

It was almost a shock, though one of the most pleasant he had ever known, when he saw the lights of Port Sanderson come up over the horizon. The curvature of this little world was very deceptive: it did not seem right that a planet with a gravity almost as great as Earth's should have a horizon so close at hand. One day, someone would have to discover what lay at this world's core to give it so great a density. Perhaps the many tunnels would help —it was an unfortunate turn of thought, but the nearness of his goal had robbed it of terror now. Indeed, the thought that he might really be in danger seemed to give his adventure a certain piquancy and heightened interest. Nothing could happen to him now, with ten minutes to go and the lights of the Port already in sight.

A few minutes later, his feelings changed abruptly when he came to the sudden bend in the road. He had forgotten the chasm that caused his detour, and added half a mile to the journey. Well, what of it? he thought stubbornly. An extra half-mile would make no difference now—another ten minutes, at the most.

It was very disappointing when the lights of the city vanished. Armstrong had not remembered the hill which the road was skirting; perhaps it was only a low ridge, scarcely noticeable in the daytime. But by hiding the

lights of the port it had taken away his chief talisman and
left him again at the mercy of his fears.

Very unreasonably, his intelligence told him, he began
to think how horrible it would be if anything happened
now, so near the end of the journey. He kept the worst of
his fears at bay for a while, hoping desperately that the
lights of the city would soon reappear. But as the minutes
dragged on, he realized that the ridge must be longer than
he imagined. He tried to cheer himself by the thought
that the city would be all the nearer when he saw it again,
but somehow logic seemed to have failed him now. For
presently he found himself doing something he had not
stooped to, even out in the waste by Carver's Pass.

He stopped, turned slowly round, and with bated
breath listened until his lungs were nearly bursting.

The silence was uncanny, considering how near he must
be to the Port. There was certainly no sound from behind
him. Of course there wouldn't be, he told himself
angrily. But he was immensely relieved. The thought of
that faint and insistent clicking had been haunting him for
the last hour.

So friendly and familiar was the noise that did reach him
at last that the anticlimax almost made him laugh aloud.
Drifting through the still air from a source clearly not
more than a mile away came the sound of a landing-field
tractor, perhaps one of the machines loading the "Canopus" itself. In a matter of seconds, thought Armstrong, he
would be around this ridge with the Port only a few
hundred yards ahead. The journey was nearly ended. In
a few moments, this evil plain would be no more than a
fading nightmare.

It seemed terribly unfair: so little time, such a small
fraction of a human life, was all he needed now. But the
gods have always been unfair to man, and now they were
enjoying their little jest. For there could be no mistaking
the rattle of monstrous claws in the darkness *ahead of him*.

The Forgotten Enemy

THE THICK FURS THUDDED SOFTLY TO THE GROUND AS PROFESsor Millward jerked himself upright on the narrow bed. This time, he was sure, it had been no dream; the freezing air that rasped against his lungs still seemed to echo with the sound that had come crashing out of the night.

He gathered the furs around his shoulders and listened intently. All was quiet again: from the narrow windows on the western walls long shafts of moonlight played upon the endless rows of books, as they played upon the dead city beneath. The world was utterly still; even in the old days the city would have been silent on such a night, and it was doubly silent now.

With weary resolution Professor Millward shuffled out of bed, and doled a few lumps of coke into the glowing brazier. Then he made his way slowly toward the nearest window, pausing now and then to rest his hand lovingly on the volumes he had guarded all these years.

He shielded his eyes from the brilliant moonlight and peered out into the night. The sky was cloudless: the sound he had heard had not been thunder, whatever it might have been. It had come from the north, and even as he waited it came again.

Distance had softened it, distance and the bulk of the hills that lay beyond London. It did not race across the sky with the wantonness of thunder, but seemed to come from a single point far to the north. It was like no natural sound that he had ever heard, and for a moment he dared to hope again.

Only Man, he was sure, could have made such a sound. Perhaps the dream that had kept him here among these treasures of civilization for more than twenty years would soon be a dream no longer. Men were returning to Eng-

41

land, blasting their way through the ice and snow with the weapons that science had given them before the coming of the Dust. It was strange that they should come by land, and from the north, but he thrust aside any thoughts that would quench the newly kindled flame of hope.

Three hundred feet below, the broken sea of snow-covered roofs lay bathed in the bitter moonlight. Miles away the tall stacks of Battersea Power Station glimmered like thin white ghosts against the night sky. Now that the dome of St. Paul's had collapsed beneath the weight of snow, they alone challenged his supremacy.

Professor Millward walked slowly back along the book-shelves, thinking over the plan that had formed in his mind. Twenty years ago he had watched the last heli-copters climbing heavily out of Regent's Park, the rotors churning the ceaselessly falling snow. Even then, when the silence had closed around him, he could not bring himself to believe that the North had been abandoned for-ever. Yet already he had waited a whole generation, among the books to which he had dedicated his life.

In those early days he had sometimes heard, over the radio which was his only contact with the South, of the struggle to colonize the now-temperate lands of the Equa-tor. He did not know the outcome of that far-off battle, fought with desperate skill in the dying jungles and across deserts that had already felt the first touch of snow. Per-haps it had failed; the radio had been silent now for fif-teen years or more. Yet if men and machines were indeed returning from the north—of all directions—he might again be able to hear their voices as they spoke to one an-other and to the lands from which they had come.

Professor Millward left the University building per-haps a dozen times a year, and then only through sheer necessity. Over the past two decades he had collected everything he needed from the shops in the Bloomsbury area, for in the final exodus vast supplies of stocks had been left behind through lack of transport. In many ways, indeed, his life could be called luxurious: no professor of English literature had ever been clothed in such garments as those he had taken from an Oxford Street furrier's.

The sun was blazing from a cloudless sky as he shouldered his pack and unlocked the massive gates. Even ten years ago packs of starving dogs had hunted in this area, and though he had seen none for years he was still cautious and always carried a revolver when he went into the open.

The sunlight was so brilliant that the reflected glare hurt his eyes; but it was almost wholly lacking in heat. Although the belt of cosmic dust through which the Solar System was now passing had made little visible difference to the sun's brightness, it had robbed it of all strength. No one knew whether the world would swim out into the warmth again in ten or a thousand years, and civilization had fled southward in search of lands where the word "summer" was not an empty mockery.

The latest drifts had packed hard and Professor Millward had little difficulty in making the journey to Tottenham Court Road. Sometimes it had taken him hours of floundering through the snow, and one year he had been sealed in his great concrete watchtower for nine months.

He kept away from the houses with their dangerous burdens of snow and their Damoclean icicles, and went north until he came to the shop he was seeking. The words above the shattered windows were still bright: "Jenkins & Sons. Radio and Electrical. Television A Specialty."

Some snow had drifted through a broken section of roofing, but the little upstairs room had not altered since his last visit a dozen years ago. The all-wave radio still stood on the table, and empty tins scattered on the floor spoke mutely of the lonely hours he had spent here before all hope had died. He wondered if he must go through the same ordeal again.

Professor Millward brushed the snow from the copy of *The Amateur Radio Handbook for 1965*, which had taught him what little he knew about wireless. The testmeters and batteries were still lying in their half-remembered places, and to his relief some of the batteries still held their charge. He searched through the stock until he had built up the necessary power supplies, and checked the radio as well as he could. Then he was ready.

It was a pity that he could never send the manufacturers the testimonial they deserved. The faint "hiss" from the speaker brought back memories of the B.B.C., of the nine o'clock news and symphony concerts, of all the things he had taken for granted in a world that was gone like a dream. With scarcely controlled impatience he ran across the wave-bands, but everywhere there was nothing save that omnipresent hiss. That was disappointing, but no more: he remembered that the real test would come at night. In the meantime he would forage among the surrounding shops for anything that might be useful.

It was dusk when he returned to the little room. A hundred miles above his head, tenuous and invisible, the Heaviside Layer would be expanding outward toward the stars as the sun went down. So it had done every evening for millions of years, and for half a century only, Man had used it for his own purposes, to reflect around the world his messages of hate or peace, to echo with trivialities or to sound with music once called immortal.

Slowly, with infinite patience, Professor Millward began to traverse the shortwave bands that a generation ago had been a babel of shouting voices and stabbing morse. Even as he listened, the faint hope he had dared to cherish began to fade within him. The city itself was no more silent than the once-crowded oceans of ether. Only the faint crackle of thunderstorms half the world away broke the intolerable stillness. Man had abandoned his latest conquest.

Soon after midnight the batteries faded out. Professor Millward did not have the heart to search for more, but curled up in his furs and fell into a troubled sleep. He got what consolation he could from the thought that if he had not proved his theory, he had not disproved it either.

The heatless sunlight was flooding the lonely white road when he began the homeward journey. He was very tired, for he had slept little and his sleep had been broken by the recurring fantasy of rescue.

The silence was suddenly broken by the distant thunder that came rolling over the white roofs. It came—there could be no doubt now—from beyond the northern hills that had once been London's playground. From the buildings on either side little avalanches of snow went swishing out into the wide street; then the silence returned.

Professor Millward stood motionless, weighing, considering, analyzing. The sound had been too long-drawn to be an ordinary explosion—he was dreaming again—it was nothing less than the distant thunder of an atomic bomb, burning and blasting away the snow a million tons at a time. His hopes revived, and the disappointments of the night began to fade.

That momentary pause almost cost him his life. Out of a side-street something huge and white moved suddenly into his field of vision. For a moment his mind refused to accept the reality of what he saw; then the paralysis left him and he fumbled desperately for his futile revolver. Padding toward him across the now, swinging its head from side to side with a hypnotic, serpentine motion, was a huge polar bear.

He dropped his belongings and ran, floundering over the snow toward the nearest buildings. Providentially the Underground entrance was only fifty feet away. The steel grille was closed, but he remembered breaking the lock many years ago. The temptation to look back was almost intolerable, for he could hear nothing to tell how near his pursuer was. For one frightful moment the iron lattice resisted his numbed fingers. Then it yielded reluctantly and he forced his way through the narrow opening.

Out of his childhood there came a sudden, incongruous memory of an albino ferret he had once seen weaving its body ceaselessly across the wire netting of its cage. There was the same reptile grace in the monstrous shape, almost twice as high as a man, that reared itself in baffled fury against the grille. The metal bowed but did not yield beneath the pressure; then the bear dropped to the ground, grunted softly and padded away. It slashed once or twice at the fallen haversack, scattering a few tins of food into the snow, and vanished as silently as it had come.

A very shaken Professor Millward reached the University three hours later, after moving in short bounds from one refuge to the next. After all these years he was no longer alone in the city. He wondered if there were other visitors, and that same night he knew the answer. Just before dawn he heard, quite distinctly, the cry of a wolf from somewhere in the direction of Hyde Park.

By the end of the week he knew that the animals of the North were on the move. Once he saw a reindeer running southward, pursued by a pack of silent wolves, and sometimes in the night there were sounds of deadly conflict. He was amazed that so much life still existed in the white wilderness between London and the Pole. Now something was driving it southward, and the knowledge brought him a mounting excitement. He did not believe that these fierce survivors would flee from anything save Man.

The strain of waiting was beginning to affect Professor Millward's mind, and for hours he would sit in the cold sunlight, his furs wrapped around him, dreaming of rescue and thinking of the way in which men might be returning to England. Perhaps an expedition had come from North America across the Atlantic ice. It might have been years upon its way. But why had it come so far north? His favorite theory was that the Atlantic ice-packs were not safe enough for heavy traffic further to the south.

One thing, however, he could not explain to his satisfaction. There had been no air reconnaissance; it was hard to believe that the art of flight had been lost so soon.

Sometimes he would walk along the ranks of books, whispering now and then to a well-loved volume. There were books here that he had not dared to open for years, they reminded him so poignantly of the past. But now, as the days grew longer and brighter, he would sometimes take down a volume of poetry and re-read his old favorites. Then he would go to the tall windows and shout the magic words over the rooftops, as if they would break the spell that had gripped the world.

It was warmer now, as if the ghosts of lost summers had returned to haunt the land. For whole days the temperature rose above freezing, while in many places flowers were breaking through the snow. Whatever was approaching from the north was nearer, and several times a day that enigmatic roar would go thundering over the city, sending the snow sliding upon a thousand roofs.

There were strange, grinding undertones that Professor Millward found baffling and even ominous. At times it was almost as if he were listening to the clash of mighty armies, and sometimes a mad but dreadful thought came into his mind and would not be dismissed. Often he would wake in the night and imagine he heard the sound of mountains moving to the sea.

So the summer wore away, and as the sound of that distant battle drew steadily nearer Professor Millward was the prey of ever more violently alternating hopes and fears. Although he saw no more wolves or bears—they seemed to have fled southward—he did not risk leaving the safety of his fortress. Every morning he would climb to the highest window of the tower and search the northern horizon with field-glasses. But all he ever saw was the stubborn retreat of the snows above Hampstead, as they fought their bitter rearguard action against the sun.

His vigil ended with the last days of the brief summer. The grinding thunder in the night had been nearer than ever before, but there was still nothing to hint at its real distance from the city. Professor Millward felt no premonition as he climbed to the narrow window and raised his binoculars to the northern sky.

As a watcher from the walls of some threatened fortress might have seen the first sunlight glinting on the spears of an advancing army, so in that moment Professor Millward knew the truth. The air was crystal-clear, and the hills were sharp and brilliant against the cold blue of the sky. They had lost almost all their snow. Once he would have rejoiced at that, but it meant nothing now.

Overnight, the enemy he had forgotten had conquered the last defenses and was preparing for the final onslaught. As he saw that deadly glitter along the crest of the doomed hills, Professor Millward understood at last the sound he had heard advancing for so many months. It was little wonder he had dreamed of mountains on the march.

Out of the North, their ancient home, returning in triumph to the lands they had once possessed, the glaciers had come again.

Technical Error

IT WAS ONE OF THOSE ACCIDENTS FOR WHICH NO ONE COULD
be blamed. Richard Nelson had been in and out of the
generator pit a dozen times, taking temperature readings
to make sure that the unearthly chill of liquid helium was
not seeping through the insulation. This was the first generator in the world to use the principle of superconduc-
tivity. The windings of the immense stator had been im-
mersed in a helium bath, and the miles of wire now had a
resistance too small to be measured by any means known
to man.

Nelson noted with satisfaction that the temperature had
not fallen further than expected. The insulation was doing
its work; it would be safe to lower the rotor into the pit.
That thousand-ton cylinder was now hanging fifty feet
above Nelson's head, like the business end of a mammoth
drop hammer. He and everyone else in the power station
would feel much happier when it had been lowered onto
its bearings and keyed into the turbine shaft.

Nelson put away his notebook and started to walk
toward the ladder. At the geometric center of the pit, he
made his appointment with destiny.

The load on the power network had been steadily increasing for the last hour, while the zone of twilight swept
across the continent. As the last rays of sunlight faded
from the clouds, the miles of mercury arcs along the great
highways sprang into life. By the million, fluorescent
tubes began to glow in the cities; housewives switched on
their radio-cookers to prepare the evening meal. The
needles of the megawattmeters began to creep up the
scales.

These were the normal loads. But on a mountain three
hundred miles to the south a giant cosmic ray analyzer

was being rushed into action to await the expected shower from the new supernova in Capricornus, which the astronomers had detected only an hour before. Soon the coils of its five-thousand-ton magnets began to drain their enormous currents from the thyratron converters.

A thousand miles to the west, fog was creeping toward the greatest airport in the hemisphere. No one worried much about fog, now, when every plane could land on its own radar in zero visibility, but it was nicer not to have it around. So the giant dispersers were thrown into operation, and nearly a thousand megawatts began to radiate into the night, coagulating the water droplets and clearing great swaths through the banks of mist.

The meters in the power station gave another jump, and the engineer on duty ordered the stand-by generators into action. He wished the big, new machine was finished; then there would be no more anxious hours like these. But he thought he could handle the load. Half an hour later the Meteorological Bureau put out a general frost warning over the radio. Within sixty seconds, more than a million electric fires were switched on in anticipation. The meters passed the danger mark and went on soaring.

With a tremendous crash three giant circuit breakers leaped from their contacts. Their arcs died under the fierce blast of the helium jets. Three circuits had opened— but the fourth breaker had failed to clear. Slowly, the great copper bars began to glow cherry-red. The acrid smell of burning insulation filled the air and molten metal dripped heavily to the floor below, solidifying at once on the concrete slabs. Suddenly the conductors sagged as the load ends broke away from their supports. Brilliant green arcs of burning copper flamed and died as the circuit was broken. The free ends of the enormous conductors fell perhaps ten feet before crashing into the equipment below. In a fraction of a second they had welded themselves across the lines that led to the new generator.

Forces greater than any yet produced by man were at war in the windings of the machine. There was no resistance to oppose the current, but the inductance of the tremendous windings delayed the moment of peak intensity. The current rose to a maximum in an immense surge that lasted several seconds. At that instant, Nelson reached the center of the pit.

Then the current tried to stabilize itself, oscillating wildly between narrower and narrower limits. But it never reached its steady state; somewhere, the overriding safety devices came into operation and the circuit that should never have been made was broken again. With a last dying spasm, almost as violent as the first, the current swiftly ebbed away. It was all over.

When the emergency lights came on again, Nelson's assistant walked to the lip of the rotor pit. He didn't know what had happened, but it must have been serious. Nelson, fifty feet down, must have been wondering what it was all about.

"Hello, Dick!" he shouted. "Have you finished? We'd better see what the trouble is."

There was no reply. He leaned over the edge of the great pit and peered into it. The light was very bad, and the shadow of the rotor made it difficult to see what was below. At first it seemed that the pit was empty, but that was ridiculous; he had seen Nelson enter it only a few minutes ago. He called again.

"Hello! You all right, Dick?"

Again no reply. Worried now, the assistant began to descend the ladder. He was halfway down when a curious noise, like a toy balloon bursting very far away, made him look over his shoulder. Then he saw Nelson, lying at the center of the pit on the temporary woodwork covering the turbine shaft. He was very still, and there seemed something altogether wrong about the angle at which he was lying.

Ralph Hughes, chief physicist, looked up from his littered desk as the door opened. Things were slowly returning to normal after the night's disasters. Fortunately, the trouble had not affected his department much, for the generator was unharmed. He was glad he was not the chief engineer: Murdock would still be snowed under with paperwork. The thought gave Dr. Hughes considerable satisfaction.

"Hello, Doc," he greeted the visitor. "What brings you here? How's your patient getting on?"

Doctor Sanderson nodded briefly. "He'll be out of hospital in a day or so. But I want to talk to you about him."

"I don't know the fellow—I never go near the plant, except when the Board goes down on its collective knees and asks me to. After all, Murdock's paid to run the place."

Sanderson smiled wryly. There was no love lost between the chief engineer and the brilliant young physicist. Their personalities were too different, and there was the inevitable rivalry between theoretical expert and "practical" man.

"I think this is up your street, Ralph. At any rate, it's beyond me. You've heard what happened to Nelson?"

"He was inside my new generator when the power was shot into it, wasn't he?"

"That's correct. His assistant found him suffering from shock when the power was cut off again."

"What kind of shock? It couldn't have been electric; the windings are insulated, of course. In any case, I gather that he was in the center of the pit when they found him."

"That's quite true. We don't know what happened. But he's now come round and seems none the worse—apart from one thing." The doctor hesitated a moment as if choosing his words carefully.

"Well, go on! Don't keep me in suspense!"

"I left Nelson as soon as I saw he would be quite safe, but about an hour later Matron called me up to say he wanted to speak to me urgently. When I got to the ward he was sitting up in bed looking at a newspaper with a very puzzled expression. I asked him what was the matter. He answered, 'Something's happened to me, Doc.' So I said, 'Of course it has, but you'll be out in a couple of days.' He shook his head; I could see there was a worried look in his eyes. He picked up the paper he had been looking at and pointed to it. 'I can't read any more,' he said.

"I diagnosed amnesia and thought: This is a nuisance! Wonder what else he's forgotten? Nelson must have read my expression, for he went on to say, 'Oh, I still know the letters and words—but they're the wrong way round! I think something must have happened to my eyes.' He held up the paper again. 'This looks exactly as if I'm seeing it in a mirror,' he said. 'I can spell out each word separately, a letter at a time. Would you get me a looking glass? I want to try something.'

"I did. He held the paper to the glass and looked at the reflection. Then he started to read aloud, at normal speed. But that's a trick anyone can learn—compositors have to do it with type—and I wasn't impressed. On the other hand, I couldn't see why an intelligent fellow like Nelson should put over an act like that. So I decided to humor him, thinking the shock must have given his mind a bit of a twist. I felt quite certain he was suffering from some delusion, though he seemed perfectly normal.

"After a moment he put the paper away and said, 'Well, Doc., what do you make of that?' I didn't know quite what to say without hurting his feelings, so I passed the buck and said, 'I think I'll have to hand you over to Dr. Humphries, the psychologist. It's rather outside my province.' Then he made some remark about Dr. Humphries and his intelligence tests, from which I gathered he had already suffered at his hands."

"That's correct," interjected Hughes. "All the men are grilled by the Psychology Department before they join the company. All the same, it's surprising what gets through," he added thoughtfully.

Dr. Sanderson smiled, and continued his story.

"I was getting up to leave when Nelson said, 'Oh, I almost forgot. I think I must have fallen on my right arm. The wrist feels badly sprained.' 'Let's look at it,' I said, bending to pick it up. 'No, the other arm,' Nelson said, and held up his left wrist. Still humoring him, I answered, 'Have it your own way. But you said your right one, didn't you?'

"Nelson looked puzzled. 'So what?' he replied. 'This *is* my right arm. My eyes may be queer, but there's no argument about that. There's my wedding ring to prove it. I've not been able to get the darned thing off for five years.'

"That shook me rather badly. Because you see, it was his left arm he was holding up, and his left hand that had the ring on it. I could see that what he said was quite true. The ring would have to be cut to get it off again. So I said, 'Have you any distinctive scars?' He answered, 'Not that I can remember.'

" 'Any dental fillings?' "

" 'Yes, quite a few.' "

"We sat looking at each other in silence while a nurse went to fetch Nelson's records. 'Gazed at each other with a wild surmise' is just about how a novelist might put it. Before the nurse returned, I was seized with a bright idea. It was a fantastic notion, but the whole affair was becoming more and more outrageous. I asked Nelson if I could see the things he had been carrying in his pockets. Here they are."

Dr. Sanderson produced a handful of coins and a small, leather-bound diary. Hughes recognized the latter at once as an Electrical Engineer's Diary; he had one in his own pocket. He took it from the doctor's hand and flicked it open at random, with that slightly guilty feeling one always has when a stranger's—still more, a friend's—diary falls into one's hands.

And then, for Ralph Hughes, it seemed that the foundations of his world were giving way. Until now he had listened to Dr. Sanderson with some detachment, wondering what all the fuss was about. But now the incontrovertible evidence lay in his own hands, demanding his attention and defying his logic.

For he could read not one word of Nelson's diary. Both the print and the handwriting were inverted, as if seen in a mirror.

Dr. Hughes got up from his chair and walked rapidly around the room several times. His visitor sat silently watching him. On the fourth circuit he stopped at the window and looked out across the lake, overshadowed by the immense white wall of the dam. It seemed to reassure him, and he turned to Dr. Sanderson again.

"You expect me to believe that Nelson has been laterally inverted in some way, so that his right and left sides have been interchanged?"

"I don't expect you to believe anything. I'm merely giving you the evidence. If you can draw any other conclusion I'd be delighted to hear it. I might add that I've checked Nelson's teeth. All the fillings have been transposed. Explain that away if you can. Those coins are rather interesting, too."

Hughes picked them up. They included a shilling, one of the beautiful new, beryl-copper crowns, and a few pence and halfpence. He would have accepted them as change without hesitation. Being no more observant than the next man, he had never noticed which way the Queen's head looked. But the lettering—Hughes could picture the consternation at the Mint if these curious coins ever came to its notice. Like the diary, they too had been laterally inverted.

Dr. Sanderson's voice broke into his reverie.

"I've told Nelson not to say anything about this. I'm going to write a full report; it should cause a sensation when it's published. But we want to know how this has happened. As you are the designer of the new machine, I've come to you for advice."

Dr. Hughes did not seem to hear him. He was sitting at his desk with his hands outspread, little fingers touching. For the first time in his life he was thinking seriously about the difference between left and right.

Dr. Sanderson did not release Nelson from hospital for several days, during which he was studying his peculiar patient and collecting material for his report. As far as he could tell, Nelson was perfectly normal, apart from his inversion. He was learning to read again, and his progress was swift after the initial strangeness had worn off. He would probably never again use tools in the same way that he had done before the accident; for the rest of his life, the world would think him left-handed. However, that would not handicap him in any way.

Dr. Sanderson had ceased to speculate about the cause of Nelson's condition. He knew very little about electricity; that was Hughes's job. He was quite confident that the physicist would produce the answer in due course; he had always done so before. The company was not a philanthropic institution, and it had good reason for retaining Hughes's services. The new generator, which would be running within a week, was his brain-child, though he had had little to do with the actual engineering details.

Dr. Hughes himself was less confident. The magnitude of the problem was terrifying; for he realized, as Sanderson did not, that it involved utterly new regions of science. He knew that there was only one way in which an object could become its own mirror image. But how could so fantastic a theory be proved?

He had collected all available information on the fault that had energized the great armature. Calculations had given an estimate of the currents that had flowed through the coils for the few seconds they had been conducting. But the figures were largely guesswork; he wished he could repeat the experiment to obtain accurate data. It would be amusing to see Murdock's face if he said, "Mind if I throw a perfect short across generators One to Ten sometime this evening?" No, that was definitely out.

It was lucky he still had the working model. Tests on it had given some ideas of the field produced at the generator's center, but their magnitudes were a matter of conjecture. They must have been enormous. It was a miracle that the windings had stayed in their slots. For nearly a month Hughes struggled with his calculations and wandered through regions of atomic physics he had carefully avoided since he left the university. Slowly the complete theory began to evolve in his mind; he was a long way from the final proof, but the road was clear. In another month he would have finished.

The great generator itself, which had dominated his thoughts for the past year, now seemed trivial and unimportant. He scarcely bothered to acknowledge the congratulations of his colleagues when it passed its final tests and began to feed its millions of kilowatts into the system. They must have thought him a little strange, but he had always been regarded as somewhat unpredictable. It was expected of him; the company would have been disappointed if its tame genius possessed no eccentricities.

A fortnight later, Dr. Sanderson came to see him again. He was in a grave mood.

"Nelson's back in the hospital," he announced. "I was wrong when I said he'd be O.K."

"What's the matter with him?" asked Hughes in surprise.

"He's starving to death."

"Starving? What on earth do you mean?"

Dr. Sanderson pulled a chair up to Hughes's desk and sat down.

"I haven't bothered you for the past few weeks," he began, "because I knew you were busy on your own theories. I've been watching Nelson carefully all this time, and writing up my report. At first, as I told you, he seemed perfectly normal. I had no doubt that everything would be all right.

"Then I noticed that he was losing weight. It was some time before I was certain of it; then I began to observe other, more technical symptoms. He started to complain of weakness and lack of concentration. He had all the signs of vitamin deficiency. I gave him special vitamin concentrates, but they haven't done any good. So I've come to have another talk with you."

Hughes looked baffled, then annoyed. "But hang it all, you're the doctor!"

"Yes, but this theory of mine needs some support. I'm only an unknown medico—no one would listen to me until it was too late. For Nelson is dying, and I think I know why. . . ."

Sir Robert had been stubborn at first, but Dr. Hughes had had his way, as he always did. The members of the Board of Directors were even now filing into the conference room, grumbling and generally making a fuss about the extraordinary general meeting that had just been called. Their perplexity was still further increased when they heard that Hughes was going to address them. They all knew the physicist and his reputation, but he was a scientist and they were businessmen. What was Sir Robert planning?

Dr. Hughes, the cause of all the trouble, felt annoyed with himself for being nervous. His opinion of the Board of Directors was not flattering, but Sir Robert was a man he could respect, so there was no reason to be afraid of them. It was true that they might consider him mad, but his past record would take care of that. Mad or not, he was worth thousands of pounds to them.

Dr. Sanderson smiled encouragingly at him as he walked into the conference room. The smile was not very successful, but it helped. Sir Robert had just finished speaking. He picked up his glasses in that nervous way he had, and coughed deprecatingly. Not for the first time, Hughes wondered how such an apparently timid old man could rule so vast a commercial empire.

"Well, here is Dr. Hughes, gentlemen. He will—ahem—explain everything to you. I have asked him not to be too technical. You are at liberty to interrupt him if he ascends into the more rarefied stratosphere of higher mathematics. Dr. Hughes . . ."

Slowly at first, and then more quickly as he gained the confidence of his audience, the physicist began to tell his story. Nelson's diary drew a gasp of amazement from the Board, and the inverted coins proved fascinating curiosities. Hughes was glad to see that he had aroused the interest of his listeners. He took a deep breath and made the plunge he had been fearing.

"You have heard what has happened to Nelson, gentlemen, but what I am going to tell you now is even more startling. I must ask you for your very close attention."

He picked up a rectangular sheet of notepaper from the conference table, folded it along a diagonal and tore it along the fold.

"Here we have two right-angled triangles with equal sides. I lay them on the table—so." He placed the paper triangles side by side on the table, with their hypotenuses touching, so that they formed a kite-shaped figure. "Now, as I have arranged them, each triangle is the mirror image of the other. You can imagine that the plane of the mirror is along the hypotenuse. This is the point I want you to notice. As long as I keep the triangles in the plane of the table, I can slide them around as much as I like, but I can never place one so that it exactly covers the other. Like a pair of gloves, they are not interchangeable although their dimensions are identical."

He paused to let that sink in. There were no comments, so he continued.

"Now, if I pick up one of the triangles, turn it over in the air and put it down again, the two are no longer mirror images, but have become completely identical—so." He suited the action to the words. "This may seem very elementary; in fact, it is so. But it teaches us one very important lesson. The triangles on the table were flat objects, restricted to two dimensions. To turn one into its mirror image I had to lift it up and rotate it in the third dimension. Do you see what I am driving at?"

He glanced round the table. One or two of the directors nodded slowly in dawning comprehension.

"Similarly, to change a solid, three-dimensional body, such as a man, into its analogue or mirror image, it must be rotated in a fourth dimension. I repeat—a fourth dimension."

There was a strained silence. Someone coughed, but it was a nervous, not a skeptical cough.

"Four-dimensional geometry, as you know"—he'd be surprised if they did—"has been one of the major tools of mathematics since before the time of Einstein. But until now it has always been a mathematical fiction, having no real existence in the physical world. It now appears that the unheard-of currents, amounting to millions of amperes, which flowed momentarily in the windings of our generator must have produced a certain extension into four dimensions, for a fraction of a second and in a volume large enough to contain a man. I have been making some calculations and have been able to satisfy myself that a 'hyperspace' about ten feet on a side was, in fact, generated: a matter of some ten thousand quartic—not cubic!—feet. Nelson was occupying that space. The sudden collapse of the field when the circuit was broken caused the rotation of the space, and Nelson was inverted.

"I must ask you to accept this theory, as no other explanation fits the facts. I have the mathematics here if you wish to consult them."

He waved the sheets in front of his audience, so that the directors could see the imposing array of equations. The technique worked—it always did. They cowered visibly. Only McPherson, the secretary, was made of sterner stuff. He had had a semi-technical education and still read a good deal of popular science, which he was fond of airing whenever he had the opportunity. But he was intelligent and willing to learn, and Dr. Hughes had often spent official time discussing some new scientific theory with him.

"You say that Nelson has been rotated in the Fourth Dimension; but I thought Einstein had shown that the Fourth Dimension was time."

Hughes groaned inwardly. He had been anticipating this red herring.

"I was referring to an additional dimension of space," he explained patiently. "By that I mean a dimension, or direction, at right-angles to our normal three. One can call it the Fourth Dimension if one wishes. With certain reservations, time may also be regarded as a dimension. As we normally regard space as three-dimensional, it is then customary to call time the Fourth Dimension. But the label is arbitrary. As I'm asking you to grant me four dimensions of space, we must call time the Fifth Dimension."

"Five Dimensions! Good Heavens!" exploded someone further down the table.

Dr. Hughes could not resist the opportunity. "Space of several million dimensions has been frequently postulated in sub-atomic physics," he said quietly.

There was a stunned silence. No one, not even McPherson, seemed inclined to argue.

"I now come to the second part of my account," continued Dr. Hughes. "A few weeks after his inversion we found that there was something wrong with Nelson. He was taking food normally, but it didn't seem to nourish him properly. The explanation has been given by Dr. Sanderson, and leads us into the realms of organic chemistry. I'm sorry to be talking like a textbook, but you will soon realize how vitally important this is to the company. And you also have the satisfaction of knowing that we are now all on equally unfamiliar territory."

That was not quite true, for Hughes still remembered some fragments of his chemistry. But it might encourage the stragglers.

"Organic compounds are composed of atoms of carbon, oxygen and hydrogen, with other elements, arranged in complicated ways in space. Chemists are fond of making models of them out of knitting needles and colored plasticine. The results are often very pretty and look like works of advanced art.

"Now, it is possible to have two organic compounds containing identical numbers of atoms, arranged in such a way that one is the mirror image of the other. They're called stereo-isomers, and are very common among the sugars. If you could set their molecules side by side, you would see that they bore the same sort of relationship as a right and left glove. They are, in fact, called right—or left-handed—dextro or laevo—compounds. I hope this is quite clear."

Dr. Hughes looked around anxiously. Apparently it was.

"Stereo-isomers have almost identical chemical properties," he went on, "though there are subtle differences. In the last few years, Dr. Sanderson tells me, it has been found that certain essential foods, including the new class of vitamins discovered by Professor Vandenburg, have properties depending on the arrangement of their atoms in space. In other words, gentlemen, the left-handed compounds might be essential for life, but the right-handed one would be of no value. This in spite of the fact that their chemical formulae are identical.

"You will appreciate, now, why Nelson's inversion is much more serious than we at first thought. It's not merely a matter of teaching him to read again, in which case—apart from its philosophical interest—the whole business would be trivial. He is actually starving to death in the midst of plenty, simply because he can no more assimilate certain molecules of food than we can put our right foot into a left boot.

"Dr. Sanderson has tried an experiment which has proved the truth of this theory. With very great difficulty, he has obtained the stereo-isomers of many of these vitamins. Professor Vandenburg himself synthesized them when he heard of our trouble. They have already produced a very marked improvement in Nelson's condition."

Hughes paused and drew out some papers. He thought he would give the Board time to prepare for the shock. If a man's life were not at stake, the situation would have been very amusing. The Board was going to be hit where it would hurt most.

"As you will realize, gentlemen, since Nelson was injured—if you can call it that—while he was on duty, the company is liable to pay for any treatment he may require. We have found that treatment, and you may wonder why I have taken so much of your time telling you about it. The reason is very simple. The production of the necessary stereo-isomers is almost as difficult as the extraction of radium—more so, in some cases. Dr. Sanderson tells me that it will cost over five thousand pounds a day to keep Nelson alive."

The silence lasted for half a minute; then everyone started to talk at once. Sir Robert pounded on the table, and presently restored order. The council of war had begun.

Three hours later, an exhausted Hughes left the conference room and went in search of Dr. Sanderson, whom he found fretting in his office.

"Well, what's the decision?" asked the doctor.

"What I was afraid of. They want me to re-invert Nelson."

"Can you do it?"

"Frankly, I don't know. All I can hope to do is to reproduce the conditions of the original fault as accurately as I can."

"Weren't there any other suggestions?"

"Quite a few, but most of them were stupid. McPherson had the best idea. He wanted to use the generator to invert normal food so that Nelson could eat it. I had to point out that to take the big machine out of action for this purpose would cost several millions a year, and in any case the windings wouldn't stand it more than a few times. So that scheme collapsed. Then Sir Robert wanted to know if you could guarantee there were no vitamins we'd overlooked, or that might still be undiscovered. His idea was that in spite of our synthetic diets we might not be able to keep Nelson alive after all."

"What did you say to that?"

"I had to admit it was a possibility. So Sir Robert is going to have a talk with Nelson. He hopes to persuade him to risk it; his family will be taken care of if the experiment fails."

Neither of the two men said anything for a few moments. Then Dr. Sanderson broke the silence.

"Now do you understand the sort of decision a surgeon often has to make," he said.

Hughes nodded in agreement. "It's a beautiful dilemma, isn't it? A perfectly healthy man, but it will cost two millions a year to keep him alive, and we can't even be sure of that. I know the Board's thinking of its precious balance sheet more than anything else, but I don't see any alternative. Nelson will have to take a chance."

"Couldn't you make some tests first?"

"Impossible. It's a major engineering operation to get the rotor out. We'll have to rush the experiment through when the load on the system is at minimum. Then we'll slam the rotor back, and tidy up the mess our artificial short has made. All this has to be done before the peak loads come on again. Poor old Murdock's mad as hell about it."

"I don't blame him. When will the experiment start?"

"Not for a few days, at least. Even if Nelson agrees, I've got to fix up all my gear."

No one was ever to know what Sir Robert said to Nelson during the hours they were together. Dr. Hughes was more than half prepared for it when the telephone rang and the Old Man's tired voice said, "Hughes? Get your equipment ready. I've spoken to Murdock, and we've fixed the time for Tuesday night. Can you manage by then?"

"Yes, Sir Robert."

"Good. Give me a progress report every afternoon until Tuesday. That's all."

The enormous room was dominated by the great cylinder of the rotor, hanging thirty feet above the gleaming plastic floor. A little group of men stood silently at the edge of the shadowed pit, waiting patiently. A maze of temporary wiring ran to Dr. Hughes's equipment—multibeam oscilloscopes, megawattmeters and microchronometers, and the special relays that had been constructed to make the circuit at the calculated instant.

That was the greatest problem of all. Dr. Hughes had no way of telling when the circuit should be closed; whether it should be when the voltage was at maximum, when it was at zero, or at some intermediate point on the sine wave. He had chosen the simplest and safest course. The circuit would be made at zero voltage; when it opened again would depend on the speed of the breakers.

In ten minutes the last of the great factories in the service area would be closing down for the night. The weather forecast had been favorable; there would be no abnormal loads before morning. By then, the rotor had to be back and the generator running again. Fortunately, the unique method of construction made it easy to reassemble the machine, but it would be a very close thing and there was no time to lose.

When Nelson came in, accompanied by Sir Robert and Dr. Sanderson, he was very pale. He might, thought Hughes, have been going to his execution. The thought was somewhat ill-timed, and he put it hastily aside.

There was just time enough for a last quite unnecessary check of the equipment. He had barely finished when he heard Sir Robert's quiet voice.

"We're ready, Dr. Hughes."

Rather unsteadily, he walked to the edge of the pit.

Nelson had already descended, and as he had been instructed, was standing at its exact center, his upturned face a white blob far below. Dr. Hughes waved a brief encouragement and turned away, to rejoin the group by his equipment.

He flicked over the switch of the oscilloscope and played with the synchronizing controls until a single cycle of the main wave was stationary on the screen. Then he adjusted the phasing: two brilliant spots of light moved toward each other along the wave until they had coalesced at its geometric center. He looked briefly toward Murdock, who was watching the megawattmeters intently. The engineer nodded. With a silent prayer, Hughes threw the switch.

There was the tiniest click from the relay unit. A fraction of a second later, the whole building seemed to rock as the great conductors crashed over in the switch room three hundred feet away. The lights faded, and almost died. Then it was all over. The circuit breakers, driven at almost the speed of an explosion, had cleared the line again. The lights returned to normal and the needles of the megawattmeters dropped back onto their scales.

The equipment had withstood the overload. But what of Nelson?

Dr. Hughes was surprised to see that Sir Robert, for all his sixty years, had already reached the generator. He was standing by its edge, looking down into the great pit. Slowly, the physicist went to join him. He was afraid to hurry; a growing sense of premonition was filling his mind. Already he could picture Nelson lying in a twisted heap at the center of the well, his lifeless eyes staring up at them reproachfully. Then came a still more horrible thought. Suppose the field had collapsed too soon, when the inversion was only partly completed? In another moment, he would know the worst.

There is no shock greater than that of the totally unexpected, for against it the mind has no chance to prepare its defenses. Dr. Hughes was ready for almost anything when he reached the generator. Almost, but not quite. . . .

He did not expect to find it completely empty.

What came after, he could never perfectly remember. Murdock seemed to take charge then. There was a great flurry of activity, and the engineers swarmed in to replace the giant rotor. Somewhere in the distance he heard Sir Robert saying, over and over again, "We did our best—we did our best." He must have replied, somehow, but everything was very vague. . . .

In the gray hours before the dawn, Dr. Hughes awoke from his fitful sleep. All night he had been haunted by his dreams, by weird fantasies of multi-dimensional geometry. There were visions of strange, other-worldly universes of insane shapes and intersecting planes along which he was doomed to struggle endlessly, fleeing from some nameless terror. Nelson, he dreamed, was trapped in one of those unearthly dimensions, and he was trying to reach him. Sometimes he was Nelson himself, and he imagined that he could see all around him the universe he knew, strangely distorted and barred from him by invisible walls.

The nightmare faded as he struggled up in bed. For a few moments he sat holding his head, while his mind began to clear. He knew what was happening; this was not the first time the solution of some baffling problem had come suddenly upon him in the night.

There was one piece still missing in the jigsaw puzzle that was sorting itself out in his mind. One piece only— and suddenly he had it. There was something that Nelson's assistant had said, when he was describing the original accident. It had seemed trivial at the time; until now, Hughes had forgotten all about it.

"When I looked inside the generator, there didn't seem to be anyone there, so I started to climb down the ladder. . . ."

What a fool he had been! Old McPherson had been right, or partly right, after all!

The field had rotated Nelson in the fourth dimension of space, but there had been a displacement in *time* as well. On the first occasion it had been a matter of seconds only. This time, the conditions must have been different in spite of all his care. There were so many unknown factors, and the theory was more than half guesswork.

Nelson had not been inside the generator at the end of the experiment. *But he would be.*

Dr. Hughes felt a cold sweat break out all over his body. He pictured that thousand-ton cylinder, spinning beneath the drive of its fifty million horse-power. Suppose something suddenly materialized in the space it already occupied. . . . ?

He leaped out of bed and grabbed the private phone to the power station. There was no time to lose—the rotor would have to be removed at once. Murdock could argue later.

Very gently, something caught the house by its foundations and rocked it to and fro, as a sleepy child may shake its rattle. Flakes of plaster came planing down from the ceiling; a network of cracks appeared as if by magic in the walls. The lights flickered, became suddenly brilliant, and faded out.

Dr. Hughes threw back the curtain and looked toward the mountains. The power station was invisible beyond the foothills of Mount Perrin, but its site was clearly marked by the vast column of debris that was slowly rising against the bleak light of the dawn.

The Parasite

"THERE IS NOTHING YOU CAN DO," SAID CONNOLLY, "NOTHING
at all. Why did you have to follow me?" He was standing
with his back to Pearson, staring out across the calm blue
water that led to Italy. On the left, behind the anchored
fishing fleet, the sun was setting in Mediterranean splen-
dor, incarnadining land and sky. But neither man was
even remotely aware of the beauty all around.

Pearson rose to his feet, and came forward out of the
little cafe's shadowed porch, into the slanting sunlight.
He joined Connolly by the cliff wall, but was careful not
to come too close to him. Even in normal times Connolly
disliked being touched. His obsession, whatever it might
be, would make him doubly sensitive now.

"Listen, Roy," Pearson began urgently. "We've been
friends for twenty years, and you ought to know I
wouldn't let you down this time. Besides——"

"I know. You promised Ruth."

"And why not? After all, she is your wife. She has a
right to know what's happened." He paused, choosing his
words carefully. "She's worried, Roy. Much more worried than if it was only another woman." He nearly added
the word "again," but decided against it.

Connolly stubbed out his cigarette on the flat-topped
granite wall, then flicked the white cylinder out over the
sea, so that it fell twisting and turning toward the waters
a hundred feet below. He turned to face his friend.

"I'm sorry, Jack," he said, and for a moment there was
a glimpse of the familiar personality which, Pearson knew,
must be trapped somewhere within the stranger standing
at his side. "I know you're trying to be helpful, and I
appreciate it. But I wish you hadn't followed me. You'll
only make matters worse."

"Convince me of that, and I'll go away."

Connolly sighed.

"I could no more convince you than that psychiatrist you persuaded me to see. Poor Curtis! He was such a well-meaning fellow. Give him my apologies, will you?"

"I'm not a psychiatrist, and I'm not trying to cure you —whatever that means. If you like it the way you are, that's your affair. But I think you ought to let us know what's happened, so that we can make plans accordingly."

"To get me certified?"

Pearson shrugged his shoulders. He wondered if Connolly could see through his feigned indifference to the real concern he was trying to hide. Now that all other approaches seemed to have failed, the "frankly-I-don't-care" attitude was the only one left open to him.

"I wasn't thinking of that. There are a few practical details to worry about. Do you want to stay here indefinitely? You can't live without money, even on Syrene."

"I can stay at Clifford Rawnsley's villa as long as I like. He was a friend of my father's you know. It's empty at the moment except for the servants, and they don't bother me."

Connolly turned away from the parapet on which he was resting.

"I'm going up the hill before it's dark," he said. The words were abrupt, but Pearson knew that he was not being dismissed. He could follow if he pleased, and the knowledge brought him the first satisfaction he had felt since locating Connolly. It was a small triumph, but he needed it.

They did not speak during the climb; indeed, Pearson scarcely had the breath to do so. Connolly set off at a reckless pace, as if deliberately attempting to exhaust himself. The island fell away beneath them, the white villas gleamed like ghosts in the shadowed valleys, the little fishing boats, their day's work done, lay at rest in the harbor. And all around was the darkling sea.

When Pearson caught up with his friend, Connolly was sitting in front of the shrine which the devout islanders had built on Syrene's highest point. In the daytime, there would be tourists here, photographing each other or gaping at the much-advertised beauty spread beneath them, but the place was deserted now.

Connolly was breathing heavily from his exertions, yet his features were relaxed and for the moment he seemed almost at peace. The shadow that lay across his mind had lifted, and he turned to Pearson with a smile that echoed his old, infectious grin.

"He hates exercise, Jack. It always scares him away."

"And who is he?" said Pearson. "Remember, you haven't introduced us yet."

Connolly smiled at his friend's attempted humor; then his face suddenly became grave.

"Tell me, Jack," he began. "Would you say I have an overdeveloped imagination?"

"No: you're about average. You're certainly less imaginative than I am."

Connolly nodded slowly.

"That's true enough, Jack, and it should help you to believe me. Because I'm certain I could never have invented the creature who's haunting me. He really exists. I'm not suffering from paranoiac hallucinations, or whatever Dr. Curtis would call them.

"You remember Maude White? It all began with her. I met her at one of David Trescott's parties, about six weeks ago. I'd just quarreled with Ruth and was rather fed up. We were both pretty tight, and as I was staying in town she came back to the flat with me."

Pearson smiled inwardly. Poor Roy! It was always the same pattern, though he never seemed to realize it. Each affair was different to him, but to no one else. The eternal Don Juan, always seeking—always disappointed, because what he sought could be found only in the cradle or the grave, but never between the two.

"I guess you'll laugh at what knocked me out—it seems so trivial, though it frightened me more than anything that's ever happened in my life. I simply went over to the cocktail cabinet and poured out the drinks, as I've done a hundred times before. It wasn't until I'd handed one to

Maude that I realized I'd filled *three* glasses. The act was so perfectly natural that at first I didn't recognize what it meant. Then I looked wildly around the room to see where the other man was—even then I knew, somehow, that it wasn't a man. But, of course, he wasn't there. He was nowhere at all in the outside world: he was hiding deep down inside my own brain. . . ."

The night was very still, the only sound a thin ribbon of music winding up to the stars from some café in the village below. The light of the rising moon sparkled on the sea; overhead, the arms of the crucifix were silhouetted against the darkness. A brilliant beacon on the frontiers of twilight, Venus was following the sun into the west.

Pearson waited, letting Connolly take his time. He seemed lucid and rational enough, however strange the story he was telling. His face was quite calm in the moonlight, though it might be the calmness that comes after acceptance of defeat.

"The next thing I remember is lying in bed while Maude sponged my face. She was pretty frightened: I'd passed out and cut my forehead badly as I fell. There was a lot of blood around the place, but that didn't matter. The thing that really scared me was the thought that I'd gone crazy. That seems funny, now that I'm much more scared of being sane.

"*He* was still there when I woke up; he's been there ever since. Somehow I got rid of Maude—it wasn't easy—and tried to work out what had happened. Tell me, Jack, do you believe in telepathy?"

The abrupt challenge caught Pearson off his guard.

"I've never given it much thought, but the evidence seems rather convincing. Do you suggest that someone else is reading your mind?"

"It's not as simple as that. What I'm telling you now I've discovered slowly—usually when I've been dreaming or slightly drunk. You may say that invalidates the evidence, but I don't think so. At first it was the only way I could break through the barrier that separates me from

Omega—I'll tell you later why I've called him that. But now there aren't any obstacles: I know he's there all the time, waiting for me to let down my guard. Night and day, drunk or sober, I'm conscious of his presence. At times like this he's quiescent, watching me out of the corner of his eye. My only hope is that he'll grow tired of waiting, and go in search of some other victim."

Connolly's voice, calm until now, suddenly came near to breaking.

"Try and imagine the horror of that discovery: the effect of learning that every act, every thought or desire that flitted through your mind was being watched and shared by another being. It meant, of course, the end of all normal life for me. I had to leave Ruth and I couldn't tell her why. Then, to make matters worse, Maude came chasing after me. She wouldn't leave me alone, and bombarded me with letters and phone calls. It was hell. I couldn't fight both of them, so I ran away. And I thought that on Syrene, of all places, he would find enough to interest him without bothering me."

"Now I understand," said Pearson softly. "So *that's* what he's after. A kind of telepathic Peeping Tom—no longer content with mere watching. . . ."

"I suppose you're humoring me," said Connolly, without resentment. "But I don't mind, and you've summed it up pretty accurately, as you usually do. It was quite a while before I realized what his game was. Once the first shock had worn off, I tried to analyze the position logically. I thought backward from that first moment of recognition, and in the end I knew that it wasn't a sudden invasion of my mind. He'd been with me for years, so well hidden that I'd never guessed it. I expect you'll laugh at this, knowing me as you do. But I've never been altogether at ease with a woman, even when I've been making love to her, and now I know the reason. Omega has always been there, sharing my emotions, gloating over the passions he can no longer experience in his body.

"The only way I kept any control was by fighting back, trying to come to grips with him and to understand what he was. And in the end I succeeded. He's a long way away and there must be some limit to his powers. Perhaps that first contact was an accident, though I'm not sure.

"What I've told you already, Jack, must be hard enough for you to believe, but it's nothing to what I've got to say now. Yet remember—you agreed that I'm not an imaginative man, and see if you can find a flaw anywhere in this story.

"I don't know if you've read any of the evidence suggesting that telepathy is somehow independent of time. I *know* that it is. Omega doesn't belong to our age: he's somewhere in the future, immensely far ahead of us. For a while I thought he must be one of the last men—that's why I gave him his name. But now I'm not sure; perhaps he belongs to an age when there are a myriad different races of man, scattered all over the universe—some still ascending, others sinking into decay. His people, wherever and whenever they may be, have reached the heights and fallen from them into the depths the beasts can never know. There's a sense of evil about him, Jack—the real evil that most of us never meet in all our lives. Yet sometimes I feel almost sorry for him, because I know what has made him the thing he is.

"Have you ever wondered, Jack, what the human race will do when science has discovered everything, when there are no more worlds to be explored, when all the stars have given up their secrets? Omega is one of the answers. I hope he's not the only one, for if so everything we've striven for is in vain. I hope that he and his race are an isolated cancer in a still healthy universe, but I can never be sure.

"They have pampered their bodies until they are useless, and too late they have discovered their mistake. Perhaps they have thought, as some men have thought, that they could live by intellect alone. And perhaps they are immortal, and that must be their real damnation. Through the ages their minds have been corroding in their feeble bodies, seeking some release from their intolerable boredom. They have found it at last in the only way they can, by sending back their minds to an earlier, more virile age, and becoming parasites on the emotions of others.

"I wonder how many of them there are? Perhaps they explain all cases of what used to be called possession. How they must have ransacked the past to assuage their hunger! Can't you picture them, flocking like carrion crows around the decaying Roman Empire, jostling one another for the minds of Nero and Caligula and Tiberius? Perhaps Omega failed to get those richer prizes. Or perhaps he hasn't much choice and must take whatever mind he can contact in any age, transferring from that to the next whenever he has the chance.

"It was only slowly, of course, that I worked all this out. I think it adds to his enjoyment to know that I'm aware of his presence. I think he's deliberately helping—breaking down his side of the barrier. For in the end, I was able to see him."

Connolly broke off. Looking around, Pearson saw that they were no longer alone on the hilltop. A young couple, hand in hand, were coming up the road toward the crucifix. Each had the physical beauty so common and so cheap among the islanders. They were oblivious to the night around them and to any spectators, and went past without the least sign of recognition. There was a bitter smile on Connolly's lips as he watched them go.

"I suppose I should be ashamed of this, but I was wishing then that he'd leave me and go after that boy. But he won't; though I've refused to play his game any more, he's staying to see what happens."

"You were going to tell me what he's like," said Pearson, annoyed at the interruption. Connolly lit a cigarette and inhaled deeply before replying.

"Can you imagine a room without walls? He's in a kind of hollow, egg-shaped space—surrounded by blue mist that always seems to be twisting and turning, but never changes its position. There's no entrance or exit—and no gravity, unless he's learned to defy it. Because he floats in the center, and around him is a circle of short, fluted cylinders, turning slowly in the air. I think they must be machines of some kind, obeying his will. And once there was a large oval hanging beside him, with perfectly human, beautifully formed arms coming from it. It could only have been a robot, yet those hands and fingers seemed alive. They were feeding and massaging him, treating him like a baby. It was horrible. . . .

"Have you ever seen a lemur or a spectral tarsier? He's rather like that—a nightmare travesty of mankind, with huge malevolent eyes. And this is strange—it's not the way one had imagined evolution going—he's covered with a fine layer of fur, as blue as the room in which he lives. Every time I've seen him he's been in the same position, half curled up like a sleeping baby. I think his legs have completely atrophied; perhaps his arms as well. Only his brain is still active, hunting up and down the ages for its prey.

"And now you know why there was nothing you or anyone else could do. Your psychiatrists might cure me if I was insane, but the science that can deal with Omega hasn't been invented yet."

Connolly paused, then smiled wryly.

"Just because I'm sane, I realize that you can't be expected to believe me. So there's no common ground on which we can meet."

Pearson rose from the boulder on which he had been sitting, and shivered slightly. The night was becoming cold, but that was nothing to the feeling of inner helplessness that had overwhelmed him as Connolly spoke.

"I'll be frank, Roy," he began slowly. "Of course I don't believe you. But insofar as you believe in Omega yourself, he's real to you, and I'll accept him on that basis and fight him with you."

"It may be a dangerous game. How do we know what he can do when he's cornered?"

"I'll take that chance," Pearson replied, beginning to walk down the hill. Connolly followed him without argument. "Meanwhile, just what do you propose to do yourself?"

"Relax. Avoid emotion. Above all, keep away from women—Ruth, Maude, and the rest of them. That's been the hardest job. It isn't easy to break the habits of a lifetime."

"I can well believe that," replied Pearson, a little dryly. "How successful have you been so far?"

"Completely. You see, his own eagerness defeats his purpose, by filling me with a kind of nausea and self-loathing whenever I think of sex. Lord, to think that I've laughed at the prudes all my life, yet now I've become one myself!"

There, thought Pearson in a sudden flash of insight, was the answer. He would never have believed it, but Connolly's past had finally caught up with him. Omega was nothing more than a symbol of conscience, a personification of guilt. When Connolly realized this, he would cease to be haunted. As for the remarkably detailed nature of the hallucination, that was yet another example of the tricks the human mind can play in its efforts to deceive itself. There must be some reason why the obsession had taken this form, but that was of minor importance.

Pearson explained this to Connolly at some length as they approached the village. The other listened so patiently that Pearson had an uncomfortable feeling that he was the one who was being humored, but he continued grimly to the end. When he had finished, Connolly gave a short, mirthless laugh.

"Your story's as logical as mine, but neither of us can convince the other. If you're right, then in time I may returned to 'normal.' I can't disprove the possibility; I simply don't believe it. You can't imagine how real Omega is to me. He's more real than you are: if I close my eyes you're gone, but he's still there. I wish I knew what he was waiting for! I've left my old life behind; *he* knows I won't go back to it while he's there. So what's he got to gain by hanging on?" He turned to Pearson with a feverish eagerness. "That's what really frightens me, Jack. He must know what my future is—all my life must be like a book he can dip into where he pleases. So there must still be some experience ahead of me that he's waiting to savor. Sometimes—sometimes I wonder if it's my death."

They were now among the houses at the outskirts of the village, and ahead of them the nightlife of Syrene was getting into its stride. Now that they were no longer alone, there came a subtle change in Connolly's attitude. On the hilltop he had been, if not his normal self, at least friendly and prepared to talk. But now the sight of the happy, carefree crowds ahead seemed to make him withdraw into himself. He lagged behind as Pearson advanced and presently refused to come any further.

"What's the matter?" asked Pearson. "Surely you'll come down to the hotel and have dinner with me?"

Connolly shook his head.

"I can't," he said. "I'd meet too many people."

It was an astonishing remark from a man who had always delighted in crowds and parties. It showed, as nothing else had done, how much Connolly had changed. Before Pearson could think of a suitable reply, the other had turned on his heels and made off up a side-street. Hurt and annoyed, Pearson started to pursue him, then decided that it was useless.

That night he sent a long telegram to Ruth, giving what reassurance he could. Then, tired out, he went to bed.

Yet for an hour he was unable to sleep. His body was exhausted, but his brain was still active. He lay watching the patch of moonlight move across the pattern on the wall, marking the passage of time as inexorably as it must still do in the distant age that Connolly had glimpsed. Of course, that was pure fantasy—yet against his will Pearson was growing to accept Omega as a real and living threat. And in a sense Omega *was* real—as real as those other mental abstractions, the Ego and the Subconscious Mind.

Pearson wondered if Connolly had been wise to come back to Syrene. In times of emotional crisis—there had been others, though none so important as this—Connolly's reaction was always the same. He would return again to the lovely island where his charming, feckless parents had borne him and where he had spent his youth. He was seeking now, Pearson knew well enough, the contentment he had known only for one period of his life, and which he had sought so vainly in the arms of Ruth and all those others who had been unable to resist him.

Pearson was not attempting to criticize his unhappy friend. He never passed judgments; he merely observed with a bright-eyed, sympathetic interest that was hardly tolerance, since tolerance implied the relaxation of standards which he had never possessed. . . .

After a restless night, Pearson finally dropped into a sleep so sound that he awoke an hour later than usual. He had breakfast in his room, then went down to the reception desk to see if there was any reply from Ruth. Someone else had arrived in the night: two traveling cases, obviously English, were stacked in a corner of the hall, waiting for the porter to move them. Idly curious, Pearson glanced at the labels to see who his compatriot might be. Then he stiffened, looked hastily around, and hurried across to the receptionist.

"This Englishwoman," he said anxiously. "When did she arrive?"

"An hour ago, Signor, on the morning boat."

"Is she in now?"

The receptionist looked a little undecided, then capitulated gracefully.

"No, Signor. She was in a great hurry, and asked me where she could find Mr. Connolly. So I told her. I hope it was all right."

Pearson cursed under his breath. It was an incredible stroke of bad luck, something he would never have dreamed of guarding against. Maude White was a woman of even greater determination than Connolly had hinted. Somehow she had discovered where he had fled, and pride or desire or both had driven her to follow. That she had come to this hotel was not surprising; it was an almost inevitable choice for English visitors to Syrene.

As he climbed the road to the Villa, Pearson fought against an increasing sense of futility and uselessness. He had no idea what he should do when he met Connolly and Maude. He merely felt a vague yet urgent impulse to be helpful. If he could catch Maude before she reached the villa, he might be able to convince her that Connolly was a sick man and that her intervention could only do harm. Yet was this true? It was perfectly possible that a touching reconciliation had already taken place, and that neither party had the least desire to see him.

They were talking together on the beautifully laid-out lawn in front of the Villa when Pearson turned through the gates and paused for breath. Connolly was resting on a wrought-iron seat beneath a palm tree, while Maude was pacing up and down a few yards away. She was speaking swiftly; Pearson could not hear her words, but from the intonation of her voice she was obviously pleading with Connolly. It was an embarrassing situation. While Pearson was still wondering whether to go forward, Connolly looked up and caught sight of him. His face was a completely expressionless mask; it showed neither welcome nor resentment.

At the interruption, Maude spun round to see who the intruder was, and for the first time Pearson glimpsed her face. She was a beautiful woman, but despair and anger had so twisted her features that she looked like a figure from some Greek tragedy. She was suffering not only the bitterness of being scorned, but the agony of not knowing why.

Pearson's arrival must have acted as a trigger to her pent-up emotions. She suddenly whirled away from him and turned toward Connolly, who continued to watch her with lack-lustre eyes. For a moment Pearson could not see what she was doing; then he cried in horror: "Look out, Roy!"

Connolly moved with surprising speed, as if he had suddenly emerged from a trance. He caught Maude's wrist, there was a brief struggle, and then he was backing away from her, looking with fascination at something in the palm of his hand. The woman stood motionless, paralyzed with fear and shame, knuckles pressed against her mouth.

Connolly gripped the pistol with his right hand and stroked it lovingly with his left. There was a low moan from Maude.

"I only meant to frighten you, Roy! I swear it!"

"That's all right, my dear," said Connolly softly. "I believe you. There's nothing to worry about." His voice was perfectly natural. He turned toward Pearson, and gave him his old, boyish smile.

"So *this* is what he was waiting for, Jack," he said. "I'm not going to disappoint him."

"No!" gasped Pearson, white with terror. "Don't, Roy, for God's sake!"

But Connolly was beyond the reach of his friend's entreaties as he turned the pistol to his head. In that same moment Pearson knew at last, with an awful clarity, that Omega was real and that Omega would now be seeking for a new abode.

He never saw the flash of the gun or heard the feeble but adequate explosion. The world he knew had faded from his sight, and around him now were the fixed yet crawling mists of the blue room. Staring from its center—as they had stared down the ages at how many others?—were two vast and lidless eyes. They were satiated for the moment, but for the moment only.

The Fires Within

"THIS," SAID KARN SMUGLY, "WILL INTEREST YOU. JUST take a look at it!"

He pushed across the file he had been reading, and for the *nth* time I decided to ask for his transfer or, failing that, my own.

"What's it about?" I said wearily.

"It's a long report from a Dr. Matthews to the Minister of Science." He waved it in front of me. "Just read it!"

Without much enthusiasm, I began to go through the file. A few minutes later I looked up and admitted grudgingly: "Maybe you're right—this time." I didn't speak again until I'd finished. . . .

My dear Minister (the letter began). As you requested, here is my special report on Professor Hancock's experiments, which have had such unexpected and extraordinary results. I have not had time to cast it into a more orthodox form, but am sending you the dictation just as it stands.

Since you have many matters engaging your attention, perhaps I should briefly summarize our dealings with Professor Hancock. Until 1955, the Professor held the Kelvin Chair of Electrical Engineering at Brendon University, from which he was granted indefinite leave of absence to carry out his researches. In these he was joined by the late Dr. Clayton, sometime Chief Geologist to the Ministry of Fuel and Power. Their joint research was financed by grants from the Paul Fund and the Royal Society.

The Professor hoped to develop sonar as a means of precise geological surveying. Sonar, as you will know, is the acoustic equivalent of radar, and although less familiar is older by some millions of years, since bats use it very effectively to detect insects and obstacles at night. Professor Hancock intended to send high-powered supersonic pulses into the ground and to build up from the returning echoes an image of what lay beneath. The picture would be displayed on a cathode ray tube and the whole system would be exactly analagous to the type of radar used in aircraft to show the ground through cloud.

In 1957 the two scientists had achieved partial success but had exhausted their funds. Early in 1958 they applied directly to the government for a block grant. Dr. Clayton pointed out the immense value of a device which would enable us to take a kind of X-ray photo of the Earth's crust, and the Minister of Fuel gave it his approval before passing on the application to us. At that time the report of the Bernal Committee had just been published and we were very anxious that deserving cases should be dealt with quickly to avoid further criticisms. I went to see the Professor at once and submitted a favorable report; the first payment of our grant (S/543A/68) was made a few days later. From that time I have been continually in touch with the research and have assisted to some extent with technical advice.

The equipment used in the experiments is complex, but its principles are simple. Very short but extremely powerful pulses of supersonic waves are generated by a special transmitter which revolves continuously in a pool of a heavy organic liquid. The beam produced passes into the ground and "scans" like a radar beam searching for echoes. By a very ingenious time-delay circuit which I will resist the temptation to describe, echoes from any depth can be selected and so pictures of the strata under investigation can be built up on a cathode ray screen in the normal way.

When I first met Professor Hancock his apparatus was rather primitive, but he was able to show me the distribution of rock down to a depth of several hundred feet and we could see quite clearly a part of the Bakerloo Line which passed very near his laboratory. Much of the Professor's success was due to the great intensity of his supersonic bursts; almost from the beginning he was able to generate peak powers of several hundred kilowatts, nearly all of which was radiated into the ground. It was unsafe to remain near the transmitter, and I noticed that the soil became quite warm around it. I was rather surprised to see large numbers of birds in the vicinity, but soon discovered that they were attracted by the hundreds of dead worms lying on the ground.

At the time of Dr. Clayton's death in 1960, the equipment was working at a power level of over a megawatt and quite good pictures of strata a mile down could be obtained. Dr. Clayton had correlated the results with known geographical surveys, and had proved beyond doubt the value of the information obtained.

Dr. Clayton's death in a motor accident was a great tragedy. He had always exerted a stabilizing influence on the Professor, who had never been much interested in the practical applications of his work. Soon afterward I noticed a distinct change in the Professor's outlook, and a few months later he confided his new ambitions to me. I had been trying to persuade him to publish his results (he had already spent over £50,000 and the Public Accounts Committee was being difficult again), but he asked for a little more time. I think I can best explain his attitude by his own words, which I remember very vividly, for they were expressed with peculiar emphasis.

"Have you ever wondered," he said, "what the Earth really is like inside? We've only scratched the surface with our mines and wells. What lies beneath is as unknown as the other side of the Moon.

"We know that the Earth is unnaturally dense—far denser than the rocks and soil of its crust would indicate. The core may be solid metal, but until now there's been no way of telling. Even ten miles down the pressure must be thirty tons or more to the square inch and the temperature several hundred degrees. What it's like at the center staggers the imagination: the pressure must be thousands of tons to the square inch. It's strange to think that in two or three years we may have reached the Moon, but when we've got to the stars we'll still be no nearer that inferno four thousand miles beneath our feet.

"I can now get recognizable echoes from two miles down, but I hope to step up the transmitter to ten megawatts in a few months. With that power, I believe the range will be increased to ten miles; and I don't mean to stop there."

I was impressed, but at the same time I felt a little skeptical.

"That's all very well," I said, "but surely the deeper you go the less there'll be to see. The pressure will make any cavities impossible, and after a few miles there will simply be a homogeneous mass getting denser and denser."

"Quite likely," agreed the Professor. "But I can still learn a lot from the transmission characteristics. Anyway, we'll see when we get there!"

That was four months ago; and yesterday I saw the result of that research. When I answered his invitation the Professor was clearly excited, but he gave me no hint of what, if anything, he had discovered. He showed me his improved equipment and raised the new receiver from its bath. The sensitivity of the pickups had been greatly improved, and this alone had effectively doubled the range, altogether apart from the increased transmitter power. It was strange to watch the steel framework slowly turning and to realize that it was exploring regions, which, in spite of their nearness, man might never reach.

When we entered the hut containing the display equipment, the Professor was strangely silent. He switched on the transmitter, and even though it was a hundred yards away I could feel an uncomfortable tingling. Then the cathode ray tube lit up and the slowly revolving time-base drew the picture I had seen so often before. Now, however, the definition was much improved owing to the increased power and sensitivity of the equipment. I adjusted the depth control and focussed on the Underground, which was clearly visible as a dark lane across the faintly luminous screen. While I was watching, it suddenly seemed to fill with mist and I knew that a train was going through.

Presently I continued the descent. Although I had watched this picture many times before, it was always uncanny to see great luminous masses floating toward me and to know that they were buried rocks—perhaps the debris from the glaciers of fifty thousand years ago. Dr. Clayton had worked out a chart so that we could identify the various strata as they were passed, and presently I saw that I was through the alluvial soil and entering the great clay saucer which traps and holds the city's artesian water. Soon that too was passed, and I was dropping down through the bedrock almost a mile below the surface.

The picture was still clear and bright, though there was little to see, for there were now few changes in the ground structure. The pressure was already rising to a thousand atmospheres; soon it would be impossible for any cavity to remain open, for the rock itself would begin to flow. Mile after mile I sank, but only a pale mist floated on the screen, broken sometimes when echoes were returned from pockets or lodes of denser material. They became fewer and fewer as the depth increased—or else they were now so small that they could no longer be seen.

The scale of the picture was, of course, continually expanding. It was now many miles from side to side, and I felt like an airman looking down upon an unbroken cloud ceiling from an enormous height. For a moment a sense of vertigo seized me as I thought of the abyss into which I was gazing. I do not think that the world will ever seem quite solid to me again.

At a depth of nearly ten miles I stopped and looked at the Professor. There had been no alteration for some time, and I knew that the rock must now be compressed into a featureless, homogeneous mass. I did a quick mental calculation and shuddered as I realized that the pressure must be at least thirty tons to the square inch. The scanner was revolving very slowly now, for the feeble echoes were taking many seconds to struggle back from the depths.

"Well, Professor," I said, "I congratulate you. It's a wonderful achievement. But we seem to have reached the core now. I don't suppose there'll be any change from here to the center."

He smiled a little wryly. "Go on," he said. "You haven't finished yet."

There was something in his voice that puzzled and

alarmed me. I looked at him intently for a moment; his features were just visible in the blue-green glow of the cathode ray tube.

"How far down can this thing go?" I asked, as the interminable descent started again.

"Fifteen miles," he said shortly. I wondered how he knew, for the last feature I had seen at all clearly was only eight miles down. But I continued the long fall through the rock, the scanner turning more and more slowly now, until it took almost five minutes to make a complete revolution. Behind me I could hear the Professor breathing heavily, and once the back of my chair gave a crack as his fingers gripped it.

Then, suddenly, very faint markings began to reappear on the screen. I leaned forward eagerly, wondering if this was the first glimpse of the world's iron core. With agonizing slowness the scanner turned through a right angle, then another. And then——

I leaped suddenly out of my chair, cried "My God!" and turned to face the Professor. Only once before in my life had I received such an intellectual shock—fifteen years ago, when I had accidentally turned on the radio and heard of the fall of the first atomic bomb. That had been unexpected, but this was inconceivable. For on the screen had appeared a grid of faint lines, crossing and recrossing to form a perfectly symmetrical lattice.

I know that I said nothing for many minutes, for the scanner made a complete revolution while I stood frozen with surprise. Then the Professor spoke in a soft, unnaturally calm voice.

"I wanted you to see it for yourself before I said anything. That picture is now thirty miles in diameter, and those squares are two or three miles on a side. You'll notice that the vertical lines converge and the horizontal ones are bent into arcs. We're looking at part of an enormous structure of concentric rings; the center must lie many miles to the north, probably in the region of Cambridge. How much further it extends in the other direction we can only guess."

"But what *is* it, for heaven's sake?"

"Well, it's clearly artificial."

"That's ridiculous! Fifteen miles down!"

The Professor pointed to the screen again. "God knows I've done my best," he said, "but I can't convince myself that Nature could make anything like that."

I had nothing to say, and presently he continued: "I discovered it three days ago, when I was trying to find the maximum range of the equipment. I can go deeper than this, and I rather think that the structure we can see is so dense that it won't transmit my radiations any further.

"I've tried a dozen theories, but in the end I keep returning to one. We know that the pressure down there must be eight or nine thousand atmospheres, and the temperature must be high enough to melt rock. But normal matter is still almost empty space. Suppose that there is life down there—not organic life, of course, but life based on partially condensed matter, matter in which the electron shells are few or altogether missing. Do you see what I mean? To such creatures, even the rock fifteen miles down would offer no more resistance than water—and we and all our world would be as tenuous as ghosts."

"Then that thing we can see——"

"Is a city, or its equivalent. You've seen its size, so you can judge for yourself the civilization that must have built it. All the world we know—our oceans and continents and mountains—is nothing more than a film of mist surrounding something beyond our comprehension."

Neither of us said anything for a while. I remember feeling a foolish surprise at being one of the first men in the world to learn the appalling truth; for somehow I never doubted that it was the truth. And I wondered how the rest of humanity would react when the revelation came.

Presently I broke into the silence. "If you're right," I said, "why have they—whatever they are—never made contact with us?"

The Professor looked at me rather pityingly. "We think we're good engineers," he said, "but how could *we* reach *them*? Besides, I'm not at all sure that there haven't been contacts. Think of all the underground creatures and the mythology—trolls and cobalds and the rest. No, it's quite impossible—I take it back. Still, the idea *is* rather suggestive."

All the while the pattern on the screen had never changed: the dim network still glowed there, challenging our sanity. I tried to imagine streets and buildings and the creatures going among them, creatures who could make their way through the incandescent rock as a fish swims through water. It was fantastic . . . and then I remembered the incredibly narrow range of temperatures and pressures under which the human race exists. *We*, not they, were the freaks, for almost all the matter in the universe is at temperatures of thousands or even millions of degrees.

"Well," I said lamely, "what do we do now?"

The Professor leaned forward eagerly. "First we must learn a great deal more, and we must keep this an absolute secret until we are sure of the facts. Can you imagine the panic there would be if this information leaked out? Of course, the truth's inevitable sooner or later, but we may be able to break it slowly.

"You'll realize that the geological surveying side of my work is now utterly unimportant. The first thing we have to do is to build a chain of stations to find the extent of the structure. I visualize them at ten-mile intervals toward the north, but I'd like to build the first one somewhere in South London to see how extensive the thing is. The whole job will have to be kept as secret as the building of the first radar chain in the late thirties.

"At the same time, I'm going to push up my transmitter power again. I hope to be able to beam the output much more narrowly, and so greatly increase the energy concentration. But this will involve all sorts of mechanical difficulties, and I'll need more assistance."

I promised to do my utmost to get further aid, and the Professor hopes that you will soon be able to visit his laboratory yourself. In the meantime I am attaching a photograph of the vision screen, which although not as clear as the original will, I hope, prove beyond doubt that our observations are not mistaken.

I am well aware that our grant to the Interplanetary

Society has brought us dangerously near the total estimate for the year, but surely even the crossing of space is less important than the immediate investigation of this discovery which may have the most profound effects on the philosophy and the future of the whole human race.

I sat back and looked at Karn. There was much in the document I had not understood, but the main outlines were clear enough.

"Yes," I said, "this is it! Where's that photograph?"

He handed it over. The quality was poor, for it had been copied many times before reaching us. But the pattern was unmistakable and I recognized it at once.

"They were good scientists," I said admiringly. "That's Callastheon, all right. So we've found the truth at last, even if it has taken us three hundred years to do it."

"Is that surprising," asked Karn, "when you consider the mountain of stuff we've had to translate and the difficulty of copying it before it evaporates?"

I sat in silence for a while, thinking of the strange race whose relics we were examining. Only once—never again! —had I gone up the great vent our engineers had opened into the Shadow World. It had been a frightening and unforgettable experience. The multiple layers of my pressure suit had made movement very difficult, and despite their insulation I could sense the unbelievable cold that was all around me.

"What a pity it was," I mused, "that our emergence destroyed them so completely. They were a clever race, and we might have learned a lot from them."

"I don't think we can be blamed," said Karn. "We never really believed that anything could exist under those awful conditions of near-vacuum, and almost absolute zero. It couldn't be helped."

I did not agree. "I think it proves that they were the more intelligent race. After all, *they* discovered us first. Everyone laughed at my grandfather when he said that the radiation he'd detected from the Shadow World must be artificial."

Karn ran one of his tentacles over the manuscript.

"We've certainly discovered the cause of that radiation," he said. "Notice the date—it's just a year before your grandfather's discovery. The Professor must have got his grant all right!" He laughed unpleasantly. "It must have given him a shock when he saw us coming up to the surface, right underneath him."

I scarcely heard his words, for a most uncomfortable feeling had suddenly come over me. I thought of the thousands of miles of rock lying below the great city of Callastheon, growing hotter and denser all the way to the Earth's unknown core. And so I turned to Karn.

"That isn't very funny," I said quietly. "It may be our turn next."

The Awakening

MARLAN WAS BORED, WITH THE ULTIMATE BOREDOM THAT only Utopia can supply. He stood before the great window and stared down at the scudding clouds, driven by the gale that was racing past the foothills of the city. Sometimes, through a rent in the billowing white blanket, he could catch a glimpse of lakes and forests and the winding ribbon of the river that flowed through the empty land he now so seldom troubled to visit. Twenty miles away to the west, rainbow-hued in the sunlight, the upper peaks of the artificial mountain that was City Nine floated above the clouds, a dream island adrift in the cold wastes of the stratosphere. Marlan wondered how many of its inhabitants were staring listlessly across at him, equally dissatisfied with life.

There was, of course, one way of escape, and many had chosen it. But that was so obvious, and Marlan avoided the obvious above all things. Besides, while there was still a chance that life might yet hold some new experience, he would not pass through the door that led to oblivion.

Out of the mist that lay beneath him, something bright and flaming burst through the clouds and dwindled swiftly toward the deep blue of the zenith. With lack-lustre eyes, Marlan watched the ascending ship: once—how long ago!—the sight would have lifted his heart. Once he too had gone on such journeys, following the road along which Man had found his greatest adventures. But now on the twelve planets and the fifty moons there was nothing one could not find on Earth. Perhaps, if only the stars could have been reached, humanity might have avoided the cul-de-sac in which it was now trapped; there would still have remained endless vistas of exploration and discovery. But the spirit of mankind had quailed before the awful immensities of interstellar space. Man had reached the planets while he was still young, but the stars had remained forever beyond his grasp.

And yet—Marlan stiffened at the thought and stared along the twisting vapor-trail that marked the path of the departed ship—if Space had defeated him, there was still another conquest to be attempted. For a long time he stood in silent thought, while, far beneath, the storm's ragged hem slowly unveiled the buttresses and ramparts of the city, and below those, the forgotten fields and forests which had once been Man's only home.

The idea appealed to Sandrak's scientific ingenuity; it presented him with interesting technical problems which would keep him occupied for a year or two. That would give Marlan ample time to wind up his affairs, or, if necessary, to change his mind.

If Marlan felt any last-minute hesitations, he was too proud to show it as he said good-by to his friends. They had watched his plans with morbid curiosity, convinced that he was indulging in some unusually elaborate form of euthanasia. As the door of the little spaceship closed behind Marlan, they walked slowly away to resume the pattern of their aimless lives; and Roweena wept, but not for long.

While Marlan made his final preparations, the ship climbed on its automatic course, gaining speed until the Earth was a silver crescent, then a fading star lost against the greater glory of the sun. Rising upward from the plane in which the planets move, the ship drove steadily toward the stars until the sun itself had become no more than a blazing point of light. Then Marlan checked his outward speed, swinging the ship round into an orbit that made it the outermost of all the sun's children. Nothing would ever disturb it here; it would circle the sun for eternity, unless by some inconceivable chance it was captured by a wandering comet.

For the last time Marlan checked the instruments that Sandrak had built. Then he went to the innermost chamber and sealed the heavy metal door. When he opened it again, it would be to learn the secret of human destiny.

His mind was empty of all emotion as he lay on the thickly padded couch and waited for the machines to do their duty. He never heard the first whisper of gas through the vents; but consciousness went out like an ebbing tide.

Presently the air crept hissing from the little chamber, and its store of heat drained outward into the ultimate cold of space. Change and decay could never enter here; Marlan lay in a tomb that would outlast any that man had ever built on Earth, and might indeed outlast the Earth itself. Yet it was more than a tomb, for the machines it carried were biding their time, and every hundred years a circuit opened and closed, counting the centuries.

So Marlan slept, in the cold twilight beyond Pluto. He knew nothing of the life that ebbed and flowed upon Earth and its sister planets while the centuries lengthened into millennia, the millennia into eons. On the world that had once been Marlan's home, the mountains crumbled and were swept into the sea; the ice crawled down from the Poles as it had done so many times before and would do many times again. On the ocean beds the mountains of the future were built layer by layer from the falling silt, and presently rose into the light of day, and in a little while followed the forgotten Alps and Himalayas to their graves.

The sun had changed very little, all things considered, when the patient mechanism of Marlan's ship reawakened from their long sleep. The air hissed back into the chamber, the temperature slowly climbed from the verge of absolute zero to a level at which life might start again. Gently, the handling machines began the delicate series of tasks which should revitalize their master.

Yet he did not stir. During the long ages that had passed since Marlan began his sleep, something had failed among the circuits that should have awakened him. Indeed, the marvel was that so much had functioned correctly; for Marlan still eluded Death, though his servants would never recall him from his slumbers.

And now the wonderful ship remembered the commands it had been given so long ago. For a little while, as its multitudinous mechanisms slowly warmed to life, it floated inert with the feeble sunlight glinting on its walls. Then, ever more swiftly, it began to retrace the path along which it had traveled when the world was young. It did not check its speed until it was once more among the inner planets, its metal hull warming beneath the rays of the ancient unwearying sun. Here it began its search, in the temperate zone where the Earth had once circled; and here it presently found a planet it did not recognize.

The size was correct, but all else was wrong. Where were the seas that once had been Earth's greatest glory? Not even their empty beds were left: the dust of vanished continents had clogged them long ago. And where, above all, was the Moon? Somewhere in the forgotten past it had crept earthward and met its doom, for the planet was now girdled, as once only Saturn had been, by a vast, thin halo of circling dust.

For a while the robot controls searched through their electronic memories as the ship considered the situation. Then it made its decision, if a machine could have shrugged its shoulders, it would have done so. Choosing a landing place at random, it fell gently down through the thin air and came to rest on a flat plain of eroded sandstone. It had brought Marlan home; there was nothing more that it could do. If there was still life on the Earth, sooner or later it would find him.

And here, indeed, those who were now masters of Earth presently came upon Marlan's ship. Their memories were long, and the tarnished metal ovoid lying upon the sandstone was not wholly strange to them. They conferred among each other with as much excitement as their natures allowed and, using their own strange tools, began to break through the stubborn walls until they reached the chamber where Marlan slept.

In their way, they were very wise, for they could understand the purpose of Marlan's machines and could tell where they had failed in their duty. In a little while the scientists had made what repairs were necessary, though they were none too hopeful of success. The best that they could expect was that Marlan's mind might be brought, if only for a little while, back to the borders of consciousness before Time exacted its long-deferred revenge.

The light came creeping back into Marlan's brain with the slowness of a winter dawn. For ages he lay on the frontiers of self-awareness, knowing that he existed but not knowing who he was or whence he had come. Then fragments of memory returned, and fitted one by one into the intricate jigsaw of personality, until at last Marlan knew that he was—Marlan. Despite his weakness, the knowledge of success brought him a deep and burning sense of satisfaction. The curiosity that had driven him down the ages when his fellows had chosen the blissful sleep of euthanasia would soon be rewarded: he would know what manner of men had inherited the earth.

Strength returned. He opened his eyes. The light was gentle, and did not dazzle him, but for a moment all was blurred and misty. Then he saw figures looming dimly above him, and was filled with a sense of dreamlike wonder, for he remembered that he should have been alone on his return to life, with only his machines to tend him.

And now the scene came swiftly into focus, and staring back at him, showing neither enmity nor friendship, neither excitement nor indifference, were the fathomless eyes of the Watchers. The thin, grotesquely articulated figures stood around him in a close-packed circle, looking down at him across a gulf which neither his mind nor theirs could ever span.

Other men would have felt terror, but Marlan only smiled, a little sadly, as he closed his eyes forever. His questing spirit had reached its goal; he had no more riddles to ask of Time. For in the last moment of his life, as he saw those waiting round him, he knew that the ancient war between Man and insect had long ago been ended, and that Man was not the victor.

Trouble With the Natives

THE FLYING SAUCER CAME DOWN VERTICALLY THROUGH THE clouds, braked to a halt about fifty feet from the ground, and settled with a considerable bump on a patch of heather-strewn moorland.

"That," said Captain Wyxtpthll, "was a lousy landing." He did not, of course, use precisely these words. To human ears his remarks would have sounded rather like the clucking of an angry hen. Master Pilot Krtclugg unwound three of his tentacles from the control panel, stretched all four of his legs, and relaxed comfortably.

"Not my fault the automatics have packed up again," he grumbled. "But what do you expect with a ship that should have been scrapped five thousand years ago? If those cheese-paring form-fillers back at Base Planet——"

"Oh, all right! We're down in one piece, which is more than I expected. Tell Crysteel and Danstor to come in here. I want a word with them before they go."

Crysteel and Danstor were, very obviously, of a different species from the rest of the crew. They had only one pair of legs and arms, no eyes at the back of the head, and other physical deficiencies which their colleagues did their best to overlook. These very defects, however, had made them the obvious choice for this particular mission, for it had needed only a minimum of disguise to let them pass as human beings under all but the closest scrutiny.

"Now you're perfectly sure," said the Captain, "that you understand your instructions?"

"Of course," said Crysteel, slightly huffed. "This isn't the first time I've made contact with a primitive race. My training in anthropology——"

"Good. And the language?"

"Well, that's Danstor's business, but I can speak it rea-

95

sonably fluently now. It's a very simple language, and after all we've been studying their radio programs for a couple of years."

"Any other points before you go?"

"Er—there's just one matter." Crysteel hesitated slightly. "It's quite obvious from their broadcasts that the social system is very primitive, and that crime and lawlessness are widespread. Many of the wealthier citizens have to use what are called 'detectives' or 'special agents' to protect their lives and property. Now we know it's against regulations, but we were wondering . . . ."

"What?"

"Well, we'd feel much safer if we could take a couple of Mark III disrupters with us."

"Not on your life! I'd be court-martialed if they heard about it at the Base. Suppose you killed some of the natives —then I'd have the Bureau of Interstellar Politics, the Aborigines Conservancy Board, and half a dozen others after me."

"There'd be just as much trouble if *we* got killed," Crysteel pointed out with considerable emotion. "After all, you're responsible for our safety. Remember that radio play I was telling you about? It described a typical household, but there were two murders in the first half hour!"

"Oh, very well. But only a Mark II—we don't want you to do too much damage if there *is* trouble."

"Thanks a lot; that's a great relief. I'll report every thirty minutes as arranged. We shouldn't be gone more than a couple of hours."

Captain Wyxtpthll watched them disappear over the brow of the hill. He sighed deeply.

"Why," he said, "of all the people in the ship did it have to be *those* two?"

"It couldn't be helped," answered the pilot. "All these primitive races are terrified of anything strange. If they saw *us* coming, there'd be general panic and before we knew where we were the bombs would be falling on top of us. You just can't rush these things."

Captain Wyxtpthll was absentmindedly making a cat's

cradle out of his tentacles in the way he did when he was worried.

"Of course," he said, "if they don't come back I can always go away and report the place dangerous." He brightened considerably. "Yes, that would save a lot of trouble."

"And waste all the months we've spent studying it?" said the pilot, scandalized. "They won't be wasted," replied the captain, unraveling himself with a flick that no human eye could have followed. "Our report will be useful for the next survey ship. I'll suggest that we make another visit in—oh, let's say five thousand years. By then the place may be civilized—though frankly, I doubt it."

Samuel Higginsbotham was settling down to a snack of cheese and cider when he saw the two figures approaching along the lane. He wiped his mouth with the back of his hand, put the bottle carefully down beside his hedge-trimming tools, and stared with mild surprise at the couple as they came into range.

"Mornin'," he said cheerfully between mouthfuls of cheese.

The strangers paused. One was surreptitiously ruffling through a small book which, if Sam only knew, was packed with such common phrases and expressions as: "Before the weather forecast, here is a gale warning," "Stick 'em up—I've got you covered!", and "Calling all cars!" Danstor, who had no needs for these aids to memory, replied promptly enough.

"Good morning, my man," he said in his best B.B.C. accent. "Could you direct us to the nearest hamlet, village, small town or other such civilized community?"

"Eh?" said Sam. He peered suspiciously at the strangers, aware for the first time that there was something very odd about their clothes. One did not, he realized dimly, normally wear a roll-top sweater with a smart pin-striped suit of the pattern fancied by city gents. And the fellow who was still fussing with the little book was actually wearing full evening dress which would have been faultless but for the lurid green and red tie, the hob-nailed boots and the cloth cap. Crysteel and Danstor had done their best, but they had seen too many television plays. When one considers that they had no other source of information, their sartorial aberrations were at least understandable.

Sam scratched his head. Furriners, I suppose, he told himself. Not even the townsfolk got themselves up like this.

He pointed down the road and gave them explicit directions in an accent so broad that no one residing outside the range of the B.B.C.'s West Regional transmitter could have understood more than one word in three. Crysteel and Danstor, whose home planet was so far away that Marconi's first signals couldn't possibly have reached it yet, did even worse than this. But they managed to get the general idea and retired in good order, both wondering if their knowledge of English was as good as they had believed.

So came and passed, quite uneventfully and without record in the history books, the first meeting between humanity and beings from Outside.

"I suppose," said Danstor thoughtfully, but without much conviction, "that he wouldn't have done? It would have saved us a lot of trouble."

"I'm afraid not. Judging by his clothes, and the work he was obviously engaged upon, he could not have been a very intelligent or valuable citizen. I doubt if he could even have understood who we were."

"Here's another one!" said Danstor, pointing ahead.

"Don't make sudden movements that might cause alarm. Just walk along naturally, and let him speak first."

The man ahead strode purposefully toward them, showed not the slightest signs of recognition, and before they had recovered was already disappearing into the distance.

"Well!" said Danstor.

"It doesn't matter," replied Crysteel philosophically. "He probably wouldn't have been any use either."

"That's no excuse for bad manners!"

They gazed with some indignation at the retreating back of Professor Fitzsimmons as, wearing his oldest hiking outfit and engrossed in a difficult piece of atomic theory, he dwindled down the lane. For the first time, Crysteel began to suspect uneasily that it might not be as simple to make contact as he had optimistically believed.

Little Milton was a typical English village, nestling at the foot of the hills whose higher slopes now concealed so portentous a secret. There were very few people about on this summer morning, for the men were already at work and the womenfolk were still tidying up after the exhausting task of getting their lords and masters safely out of the way. Consequently Crysteel and Danstor had almost reached the center of the village before their first encounter, which happened to be with the village postman, cycling back to the office after completing his rounds. He was in a very bad temper, having had to deliver a penny postcard to Dodgson's farm, a couple of miles off his normal route. In addition, the weekly parcel of laundry which Gunner Evans sent home to his doting mother had been a lot heavier than usual, as well it might, since it contained four tins of bully beef pinched from the cookhouse.

"Excuse me," said Danstor politely.

"Can't stop," said the postman, in no mood for casual conversation. "Got another round to do." Then he was gone.

"This is really the limit!" protested Danstor. "Are they *all* going to be like this?"

"You've simply got to be patient," said Crysteel. "Remember their customs are quite different from ours; it may take some time to gain their confidence. I've had this sort of trouble with primitive races before. Every anthropologist has to get used to it."

"Hmm," said Danstor. "I suggest that we call at some of their houses. Then they won't be able to run away."

"Very well," agreed Crysteel doubtfully. "But avoid anything that looks like a religious shrine, otherwise we may get into trouble."

Old Widow Tomkins' council-house could hardly have been mistaken, even by the most inexperienced of explorers, for such an object. The old lady was agreeably excited to see two gentlemen standing on her doorstep, and noticed nothing at all odd about their clothes. Visions of unexpected legacies, of newspaper reporters asking about her 100th birthday (she was really only 95, but had managed to keep it dark) flashed through her mind. She picked up the slate she kept hanging by the door and went gaily forth to greet her visitors.

"You'll have to write it down," she simpered, holding out the slate. "I've been deaf this last twenty years."

Crysteel and Danstor looked at each other in dismay. This was a completely unexpected snag, for the only written characters they had ever seen were television program announcements, and they had never fully deciphered those. But Danstor, who had an almost photographic memory, rose to the occasion. Holding the chalk very awkwardly, he wrote a sentence which, he had reason to believe, was in common use during such breakdowns in communication.

As her mysterious visitors walked sadly away, old Mrs. Tomkins stared in baffled bewilderment at the marks on her slate. It was some time before she deciphered the characters—Danstor had made several mistakes—and even then she was little the wiser.

TRANSMISSIONS WILL BE RESUMED AS SOON AS POSSIBLE.

It was the best that Danstor could do; but the old lady never did get to the bottom of it.

They were little luckier at the next house they tried. The door was answered by a young lady whose vocabulary consisted largely of giggles, and who eventually broke down completely and slammed the door in their faces. As they listened to the muffled, hysterical laughter, Crysteel and Danstor began to suspect, with sinking hearts, that their disguise as normal human beings was not as effective as they had intended.

At Number 3, on the other hand, Mrs. Smith was only too willing to talk—at 120 words to the minute in an accent as impenetrable as Sam Higginsbotham's. Danstor made his apologies as soon as he could get a word in edgeways, and moved on.

"Doesn't *anyone* talk as they do on the radio?" he lamented. "How do they understand their own programs if they all speak like this?"

"I think we must have landed in the wrong place," said Crysteel, even his optimism beginning to fail. It sagged still further when he had been mistaken, in swift succession, for a Gallup Poll investigator, the prospective Conservative candidate, a vacuum-cleaner salesman, and a dealer from the local black market.

At the sixth or seventh attempt they ran out of housewives. The door was opened by a gangling youth who clutched in one clammy paw an object which at once hypnotized the visitors. It was a magazine whose cover displayed a giant rocket climbing upward from a crater-studded planet which, whatever it might be, was obviously not the Earth. Across the background were the words: "Staggering Stories of Pseudo-Science. Price 25 cents."

Crysteel looked at Danstor with a "Do you think what I think?" expression which the other returned. Here at last, surely, was someone who could understand them. His spirits mounting, Danstor addressed the youngster.

"I think you can help us," he said politely. "We find it very difficult to make ourselves understood here. You see, we've just landed on this planet from space and we want to get in touch with your government."

"Oh," said Jimmy Williams, not yet fully returned to Earth from his vicarious adventures among the outer moons of Saturn. "Where's your spaceship?"

"It's up in the hills; we didn't want to frighten anyone."

"Is it a rocket?"

"Good gracious no. They've been obsolete for thousands of years."

"Then how does it work? Does it use atomic power?"

"I suppose so," said Danstor, who was pretty shaky on physics. "Is there any other kind of power?"

"This is getting us nowhere," said Crysteel, impatient for once. "We've got to ask *him* questions. Try and find where there are some officials we can meet."

Before Danstor could answer, a stentorian voice came from inside the house.

"Jimmy! Who's there?"

"Two . . . men," said Jimmy, a little doubtfully. "At least, they look like men. They've come from Mars. I always said that was going to happen."

There was the sound of ponderous movements, and a lady of elephantine bulk and ferocious mien appeared from the gloom. She glared at the strangers, looked at the magazine Jimmy was carrying, and summed up the situation.

"You ought to be ashamed of yourselves!" she cried, rounding on Crysteel and Danstor. "It's bad enough having a good-for-nothing son in the house who wastes all his time reading this rubbish, without grown men coming along putting more ideas into his head. Men from Mars, indeed! I suppose you've come in one of those flying saucers!"

"But I never mentioned Mars," protested Danstor feebly.

Slam! From behind the door came the sound of violent altercation, the unmistakable noise of tearing paper, and a wail of anguish. And that was that.

"Well," said Danstor at last. "What do we try next? And why did he say we came from Mars? That isn't even the nearest planet, if I remember correctly."

"I don't know," said Crysteel. "But I suppose it's natural for them to assume that we come from some close planet. They're going to have a shock when they find the truth. Mars, indeed! That's even worse than here, from the reports I've seen." He was obviously beginning to lose some of his scientific detachment.

"Let's leave the houses for a while," said Danstor. "There must be some more people outside."

This statement proved to be perfectly true, for they had not gone much further before they found themselves surrounded by small boys making incomprehensible but obviously rude remarks.

"Should we try and placate them with gifts?" said Danstor anxiously. "That usually works among more backward races."

"Well, have you brought any?"

"No, I thought you——"

Before Danstor could finish, their tormentors took to their heels and disappeared down a side street. Coming along the road was a majestic figure in a blue uniform.

Crysteel's eyes lit up.

"A policeman!" he said. "Probably going to investigate a murder somewhere. But perhaps he'll spare us a minute," he added, not very hopefully.

P. C. Hinks eyed the strangers with some astonishment, but managed to keep his feelings out of his voice.

"Hello, gents. Looking for anything?"

"As a matter of fact, yes," said Danstor in his friendliest and most soothing tone of voice. "Perhaps you can help us. You see, we've just landed on this planet and want to make contact with the authorities."

"Eh?" said P. C. Hinks startled. There was a long pause —though not too long, for P. C. Hinks was a bright young man who had no intention of remaining a village constable all his life. "So you've just landed, have you? In a spaceship, I suppose?"

"That's right," said Danstor, immensely relieved at the absence of the incredulity, or even violence, which such announcements all too often provoked on the more primitive planets.

"Well, well!" said P. C. Hinks, in tones which he hoped would inspire confidence and feelings of amity. (Not that it mattered much if they both became violent—they seemed a pretty skinny pair.) "Just tell me what you want, and I'll see what we can do about it."

"I'm so glad," said Danstor. "You see, we've landed in this rather remote spot because we don't want to create a panic. It would be best to keep our presence known to as few people as possible until we have contacted your government."

"I quite understand," replied P. C. Hinks, glancing round hastily to see if there was anyone through whom he could send a message to his sergeant. "And what do you propose to do then?"

"I'm afraid I can't discuss our long-term policy with regard to Earth," said Danstor cagily. "All I can say is that this section of the Universe is being surveyed and opened up for development, and we're quite sure we can help you in many ways."

"That's very nice of you," said P. C. Hinks heartily. "I think the best thing is for you to come along to the station with me so that we can put through a call to the Prime Minister."

"Thank you very much," said Danstor, full of gratitude. They walked trustingly beside P. C. Hinks, despite his slight tendency to keep behind them, until they reached the village police station.

"This way, gents," said P. C. Hinks, politely ushering them into a room which was really rather poorly lit and not at all well furnished, even by the somewhat primitive standards they had expected. Before they could fully take in their surroundings, there was a "click" and they found themselves separated from their guide by a large door composed entirely of iron bars.

"Now don't worry," said P. C. Hinks. "Everything will be quite all right. I'll be back in a minute."

Crysteel and Danstor gazed at each other with a surmise that rapidly deepened to a dreadful certainty.

"We're locked in!"

"This is a prison!"

"Now what are we going to do?"

"I don't know if you chaps understand English," said a languid voice from the gloom, "but you might let a fellow sleep in peace."

For the first time, the two prisoners saw that they were not alone. Lying on a bed in the corner of the cell was a somewhat dilapidated young man, who gazed at them blearily out of one resentful eye.

"My goodness!" said Danstor nervously. "Do you suppose he's a dangerous criminal?"

"He doesn't look very dangerous at the moment," said Crysteel, with more accuracy than he guessed.

"What are *you* in for, anyway?" asked the stranger, sitting up unsteadily. "You look as if you've been to a fancy-dress party. Oh, my poor head!" He collapsed again into the prone position.

"Fancy locking up anyone as ill as this!" said Danstor, who was a kind-hearted individual. Then he continued, in English, "I don't know why we're here. We just told the policeman who we were and where we came from, and this is what's happened."

"Well, who are you?"

"We've just landed——"

"Oh, there's no point in going through all that again," interrupted Crysteel. "We'll never get anyone to believe us."

"Hey!" said the stranger, sitting up once more. "What language is that you're speaking? I know a few, but I've never heard anything like that."

"Oh, all right," Crysteel said to Danstor. "You might as well tell him. There's nothing else to do until that policeman comes back anyway."

At this moment, P. C. Hinks was engaged in earnest conversation with the superintendent of the local mental home, who insisted stoutly that all his patients were present. However, a careful check was promised and he'd call back later.

Wondering if the whole thing was a practical joke, P. C. Hinks put the receiver down and quietly made his way to the cells. The three prisoners seemed to be engaged in friendly conversation, so he tiptoed away again. It would do them all good to have a chance to cool down. He rubbed his eye tenderly as he remembered what a battle it had been to get Mr. Graham into the cell during the small hours of the morning.

That young man was now reasonably sober after the night's celebrations, which he did not in the least regret. (It was, after all, quite an occasion when your degree came through and you found you'd got Honors when you'd barely expected a Pass.) But he began to fear that he was still under the influence as Danstor unfolded his tale and waited, not expecting to be believed.

In these circumstances, thought Graham, the best thing to do was to behave as matter-of-factly as possible until the hallucinations got fed up and went away.

"If you really have a spaceship in the hills," he remarked, "surely you can get in touch with it and ask someone to come and rescue you?"

"We want to handle this ourselves," said Crysteel with dignity. "Besides, you don't know our captain."

They sounded very convincing, thought Graham. The whole story hung together remarkably well. And yet . . .

"It's a bit hard for me to believe that you can build interstellar spaceships, but can't get out of a miserable village police station."

Danstor looked at Crysteel, who shuffled uncomfortably.

"We could get out easily enough," said the anthropologist. "But we don't want to use violent means unless it's absolutely essential. You've no idea of the trouble it causes, and the reports we might have to fill in. Besides, if we do get out, I suppose your Flying Squad would catch us before we got back to the ship."

"Not in Little Milton," grinned Graham. "Especially if we could get across to the 'White Hart' without being stopped. My car is over there."

"Oh," said Danstor, his spirits suddenly reviving. He turned to his companion and a lively discussion followed. Then, very gingerly, he produced a small black cylinder from an inner pocket, handling it with much the same confidence as a nervous spinster holding a loaded gun for the first time. Simultaneously, Crysteel retired with some speed to the far corner of the cell.

It was at this precise moment that Graham knew, with a sudden icy certainty, that he was stone-sober and that the story he had been listening to was nothing less than the truth.

There was no fuss or bother, no flurry of electric sparks or colored rays—but a section of the wall three feet across dissolved quietly and collapsed into a little pyramid of sand. The sunlight came streaming into the cell as, with a great sigh of relief, Danstor put his mysterious weapon away.

"Well, come on," he urged Graham. "We're waiting for you."

There were no signs of pursuit, for P. C. Hinks was still arguing on the phone, and it would be some minutes yet before that bright young man returned to the cells and received the biggest shock of his official career. No one at the "White Hart" was particularly surprised to see Graham again; they all knew where and how he had spent the night, and expressed hope that the local Bench would deal leniently with him when his case came up.

With grave misgivings, Crysteel and Danstor climbed into the back of the incredibly ramshackle Bentley which Graham affectionately addressed as "Rose." But there was nothing wrong with the engine under the rusty bonnet, and soon they were roaring out of Little Milton at fifty miles an hour. It was a striking demonstration of the relativity of speed, for Crysteel and Danstor, who had spent the last few years traveling tranquilly through space at several million miles a second, had never been so scared in their lives. When Crysteel had recovered his breath he pulled out his little portable transmitter and called the ship.

"We're on the way back," he shouted above the roar of the wind. "We've got a fairly intelligent human being with us. Expect us in—whoops!—I'm sorry—we just went over a bridge—about ten minutes. What was that? No, of course not. We didn't have the slightest trouble. Everything went perfectly smoothly. *Good-by*."

Graham looked back only once to see how his passengers were faring. The sight was rather unsettling, for their ears and hair (which had not been glued on very firmly) had blown away and their real selves were beginning to emerge. Graham began to suspect, with some discomfort, that his new acquaintances also lacked noses. Oh well, one could grow used to anything with practice. He was going to have plenty of that in the years ahead.

The rest, of course, you all know; but the full story of the first landing on Earth, and of the peculiar circumstances under which Ambassador Graham became humanity's representative to the universe at large, has never before been recounted. We extracted the main details, with a good deal of persuasion, from Crysteel and Danstor themselves, while we were working in the Department of Extraterrestrial affairs.

It was understandable, in view of their success on Earth, that they should have been selected by their superiors to make the first contact with our mysterious and secretive neighbors, the Martians. It is also understandable, in the light of the above evidence, that Crysteel and Danstor were so reluctant to embark on this later mission, and we are not really very surprised that nothing has ever been heard of them since.

The Curse

FOR THREE HUNDRED YEARS, WHILE ITS FAME SPREAD ACROSS the world, the little town had stood here at the river's bend. Time and change had touched it lightly; it had heard from afar both the coming of the Armada and the fall of the Third Reich, and all Man's wars had passed it by.

Now it was gone, as though it had never been. In a moment of time the toil and treasure of centuries had been swept away. The vanished streets could still be traced as faint marks in the vitrified ground, but of the houses, nothing remained. Steel and concrete, plaster and ancient oak—it had mattered little at the end. In the moment of death they had stood together, transfixed by the glare of the detonating bomb. Then, even before they could flash into fire, the blast waves had reached them and they had ceased to be. Mile upon mile the ravening hemisphere of flame had expanded over the level farmlands, and from its heart had risen the twisting totem-pole that had haunted the minds of men for so long, and to such little purpose.

The rocket had been a stray, one of the last ever to be fired. It was hard to say for what target it had been intended. Certainly not London, for London was no longer a military objective. London, indeed, was no longer anything at all. Long ago the men whose duty it was had calculated that three of the hydrogen bombs would be sufficient for that rather small target. In sending twenty, they had been perhaps a little overzealous.

This was not one of the twenty that had done their work so well. Both its destination and its origin were unknown: whether it had come cross the lonely Arctic wastes or far above the waters of the Atlantic, no one could tell and there were few now who cared. Once there

109

had been men who had known such things, who had watched from afar the flight of the great projectiles and had sent their own missiles to meet them. Often that appointment had been kept, high above the Earth where the sky was black and sun and stars shared the heavens together. Then there had bloomed for a moment that indescribable flame, sending out into space a message that in centuries to come other eyes than Man's would see and understand.

But that had been days ago, at the beginning of the War. The defenders had long since been brushed aside, as they had known they must be. They had held on to life long enough to discharge their duty; too late, the enemy had learned his mistake. He would launch no further rockets; those still falling he had dispatched hours ago on secret trajectories that had taken them far out into space. They were returning now unguided and inert, waiting in vain for the signals that should lead them to their destinies. One by one they were falling at random upon a world which they could harm no more.

The river had already overflowed its banks; somewhere down its course the land had twisted beneath that colossal hammer-blow and the way to the sea was no longer open. Dust was still falling in a fine rain, as it would do for days as Man's cities and treasures returned to the world that had given them birth. But the sky was no longer wholly darkened, and in the west the sun was settling through banks of angry cloud.

A church had stood here by the river's edge, and though no trace of the building remained, the gravestones that the years had gathered round it still marked its place. Now the stone slabs lay in parallel rows, snapped off at their bases and pointing mutely along the line of the blast. Some were half flattened into the ground, others had been cracked and blistered by terrific heat, but many still bore the messages they had carried down the centuries in vain.

The light died in the west and the unnatural crimson faded from the sky. Yet still the graven words could be clearly read, lit by a steady, unwavering radiance, too faint to be seen by day but strong enough to banish night.

The land was burning: for miles the glow of its radio-activity was reflected from the clouds. Through the glimmering landscape wound the dark ribbon of the steadily widening river, and as the waters submerged the land that deadly glow continued unchanging in the depths. In a generation, perhaps, it would have faded from sight, but a hundred years might pass before life could safely come this way again.

Timidly the waters touched the worn gravestone that for more than three hundred years had lain before the vanished altar. The church that had sheltered it so long had given it some protection at the last, and only a slight discoloration of the rock told of the fires that had passed this way. In the corpse-light of the dying land, the archaic words could still be traced as the water rose around them, breaking at last in tiny ripples across the stone. Line by line the epitaph upon which so many millions had gazed slipped beneath the conquering waters. For a little while the letters could still be faintly seen; then they were gone forever.

> Good frend for Iesvs sake forbeare,
> To digg the dvst encloased heare
>   Blest be ye man yt spares thes stones,
> And cvrst be he yt moves my bones.

Undisturbed through all eternity the poet could sleep in safety now: in the silence and darkness above his head, the Avon was seeking its new outlet to the sea.

Time's Arrow

THE RIVER WAS DEAD AND THE LAKE ALREADY DYING WHEN
the monster had come down the dried-up watercourse
and turned onto the desolate mud-flats. There were not
many places where it was safe to walk, and even where
the ground was hardest the great pistons of its feet sank
a foot or more beneath the weight they carried. Sometimes it had paused, surveying the landscape with quick,
birdlike movements of its head. Then it had sunk even
deeper into the yielding soil, so that fifty million years
later men could judge with some accuracy the duration
of its halts.

For the waters had never returned, and the blazing sun
had baked the mud to rock. Later still the desert had
poured over all this land, sealing it beneath protecting
layers of sand. And later—very much later—had come
Man.

"Do you think," shouted Barton above the din, "that
Professor Fowler became a palaeontologist because he
likes playing with pneumatic drills? Or did he acquire
the taste afterward?"

"Can't hear you!" yelled Davis, leaning on his shovel
in a most professional manner. He glanced hopefully at
his watch.

"Shall I tell him it's dinnertime? He can't wear a watch
while he's drilling, so he won't know any better."

"I doubt if it will work," Barton shrieked. "He's got
wise to us now and always adds an extra ten minutes. But
it will make a change from this infernal digging."

With noticeable enthusiasm the two geologists downed
tools and started to walk toward their chief. As they approached, he shut off the drill and relative silence de-

scended, broken only by the throbbing of the compressor in the background.

"About time we went back to camp, Professor," said Davis, wristwatch held casually behind his back. "You know what cook says if we're late."

Professor Fowler, M.A., F.R.S., F.G.S., mopped some, but by no means all, of the ocher dust from his forehead. He would have passed anywhere as a typical navvy, and the occasional visitors to the site seldom recognized the Vice-President of the Geological Society in the brawny, half-naked workman crouching over his beloved pneumatic drill.

It had taken nearly a month to clear the sandstone down to the surface of the petrified mud-flats. In that time several hundred square feet had been exposed, revealing a frozen snapshot of the past that was probably the finest yet discovered by palaeontology. Some scores of birds and reptiles had come here in search of the receding water, and left their footsteps as a perpetual monument eons after their bodies had perished. Most of the prints had been identified, but one—the largest of them all—was new to science. It belonged to a beast which must have weighed twenty or thirty tons: and Professor Fowler was following the fifty-million-year-old spoor with all the emotions of a big-game hunter tracking his prey. There was even a hope that he might yet overtake it; for the ground must have been treacherous when the unknown monster went this way and its bones might still be near at hand, marking the place where it had been trapped like so many creatures of its time.

Despite the mechanical aids available, the work was very tedious. Only the upper layers could be removed by the power tools, and the final uncovering had to be done by hand with the utmost care. Professor Fowler had good reason for his insistence that he alone should do the preliminary drilling, for a single slip might cause irreparable harm.

The three men were halfway back to the main camp, jolting over the rough road in the expedition's battered jeep, when Davis raised the question that had been intriguing the younger men ever since the work had begun.

"I'm getting a distinct impression," he said, "that our neighbors down the valley don't like us, though I can't imagine why. We're not interfering with them, and they might at least have the decency to invite us over."

"Unless, of course, it *is* a war research plant," added Barton, voicing a generally accepted theory.

"I don't think so," said Professor Fowler mildly. "Because it so happens that I've just had an invitation myself. I'm going there tomorrow."

If his bombshell failed to have the expected result, it was thanks to his staff's efficient espionage system. For a moment Davis pondered over this confirmation of his suspicions; then he continued with a slight cough:

"No one else has been invited, then?"

The Professor smiled at his pointed hint. "No," he said. "It's a strictly personal invitation. I know you boys are dying of curiosity but, frankly, I don't know any more about the place than you do. If I learn anything tomorrow, I'll tell you all about it. But at least we've found out who's running the establishment."

His assistants pricked up their ears. "Who is it?" asked Barton, "My guess was the Atomic Development Authority."

"You may be right," said the Professor. "At any rate, Henderson and Barnes are in charge."

This time the bomb exploded effectively; so much so that Davis nearly drove the jeep off the road—not that that made much difference, the road being what it was.

"Henderson and Barnes? In *this* god-forsaken hole?"

"That's right," said the Professor gaily. "The invitation was actually from Barnes. He apologized for not contacting us before, made the usual excuses, and wondered if I could drop in for a chat."

"Did he say what they are doing?"

"No; not a hint."

"Barnes and Henderson?" said Barton thoughtfully. "I don't know much about them except that they're physicists. What's their particular racket?"

"They're *the* experts on low-temperature physics," answered Davis. "Henderson was Director of the Cavendish for years. He wrote a lot of letters to *Nature* not so long ago. If I remember rightly, they were all about Helium II."

Barton, who didn't like physicists and said so whenever possible, was not impressed. "I don't even know what Helium II is," he said smugly. "What's more, I'm not at all sure that I want to."

This was intended for Davis, who had once taken a physics degree in, as he explained, a moment of weakness. The "moment" had lasted for several years before he had drifted into geology by rather devious routes, and he was always harking back to his first love.

"It's a form of liquid helium that only exists at a few degrees above absolute zero. It's got the most extraordinary properties—but, as far as I can see, none of them can explain the presence of two leading physicists in this corner of the globe."

They had now arrived at the camp, and Davis brought the jeep to its normal crash-halt in the parking space. He shook his head in annoyance as he bumped into the truck ahead with slightly more violence than usual.

"These tires are nearly through. Have the new ones come yet?"

"Arrived in the 'copter this morning, with a despairing note from Andrews hoping that you'd make them last a full fortnight this time."

"Good! I'll get them fitted this evening."

The Professor had been walking a little ahead; now he dropped back to join his assistants.

"You needn't have hurried Jim," he said glumly. "It's corned beef again."

It would be most unfair to say that Barton and Davis did less work because the Professor was away. They probably worked a good deal harder than usual, since the native laborers required twice as much supervision in the Chief's absence. But there was no doubt that they managed to find time for a considerable amount of extra talking.

Ever since they had joined Professor Fowler, the two young geologists had been intrigued by the strange establishment five miles away down the valley. It was clearly a research organization of some type, and Davis had identified the tall stacks of an atomic-power unit. That, of course, gave no clue to the work that was proceeding, but it did indicate its importance. There were still only a few thousand turbo-piles in the world, and they were all reserved for major projects.

There were dozens of reasons why two great scientists might have hidden themselves in this place: most of the more hazardous atomic research was carried out as far as possible from civilization, and some had been abandoned altogether until laboratories in space could be set up. Yet it seemed odd that this work, whatever it was, should be carried out so close to what had now become the most important center of geological research in the world. It might, of course, be no more than a coincidence; certainly the physicists had never shown any interest in their compatriots so near at hand.

Davis was carefully chipping round one of the great footprints, while Barton was pouring liquid perspex into those already uncovered so that they would be preserved from harm in the transparent plastic. They were working in a somewhat absentminded manner, for each was unconsciously listening for the sound of the jeep. Professor Fowler had promised to collect them when he returned from his visit, for the other vehicles were in use elsewhere and they did not relish a two-mile walk back to camp in the broiling sun. Moreover, they wanted to have any news as soon as possible.

"How many people," said Barton suddenly, "do you think they have over there?"

Davis straightened himself up. "Judging from the buildings, not more than a dozen or so."

"Then it might be a private affair, not an ADA project at all."

"Perhaps, though it must have pretty considerable backing. Of course, Henderson and Barnes could get that on their reputations alone."

"That's where the physicists score," said Barton. "They've only got to convince some war department that they're on the track of a new weapon, and they can get a couple of million without any trouble."

He spoke with some bitterness; for, like most scientists, he had strong views on this subject. Barton's views, indeed, were even more definite than usual, for he was a Quaker and had spent the last year of the War arguing with not-unsympathetic tribunals.

The conversation was interrupted by the roar and clatter of the jeep, and the two men ran over to meet the Professor.

"Well?" they cried simultaneously.

Professor Fowler looked at them thoughtfully, his expression giving no hint of what was in his mind. "Had a good day?" he said at last.

"Come off it, Chief!" protested Davis. "Tell us what you've found out."

The Professor climbed out of the seat and dusted himself down. "I'm sorry, boys," he said with some embarrassment, "I can't tell you a thing, and that's flat."

There were two united wails of protest, but he waved them aside. "I've had a very interesting day, but I've had to promise not to say anything about it. Even now I don't know exactly what's going on, but it's something pretty revolutionary—as revolutionary, perhaps, as atomic power. But Dr. Henderson is coming over tomorrow; see what you can get out of him."

For a moment, both Barton and Davis were so overwhelmed by the sense of anticlimax that neither spoke. Barton was the first to recover. "Well, surely there's a reason for this sudden interest in our activities?"

The Professor thought this over for a moment. "Yes; it wasn't entirely a social call," he admitted. "They think I may be able to help them. Now, no more questions, unless you want to walk back to camp!"

Dr. Henderson arrived on the site in the middle of the afternoon. He was a stout, elderly man, dressed rather incongruously in a dazzling white laboratory smock and very little else. Though the garb was eccentric, it was eminently practical in so hot a climate.

Davis and Barton were somewhat distant when Professor Fowler introduced them; they still felt that they had been snubbed and were determined that their visitor should understand their feelings. But Henderson was so obviously interested in their work that they soon thawed, and the Professor left them to show him round the excavations while he went to supervise the natives.

The physicist was greatly impressed by the picture of the world's remote past that lay exposed before his eyes. For almost an hour the two geologists took him over the workings yard by yard, talking of the creatures who had gone this way and speculating about future discoveries. The track which Professor Fowler was following now lay in a wide trench running away from the main excavation, for he had dropped all other work to investigate it. At its end the trench was no longer continuous: to save time, the Professor had begun to sink pits along the line of the footprints. The last sounding had missed altogether, and further digging had shown that the great reptile had made a sudden change of course.

"This is the most interesting bit," said Barton to the slightly wilting physicist. "You remember those earlier places where it had stopped for a moment to have a look around? Well, here it seems to have spotted something and has gone off in a new direction at a run, as you can see from the spacing."

"I shouldn't have thought such a brute *could* run."

"Well, it was probably a pretty clumsy effort, but you can cover quite a bit of ground with a fifteen-foot stride. We're going to follow it as far as we can. We may even find what it was chasing. I think the Professor has hopes of discovering a trampled battlefield with the bones of the victim still around. That would make everyone sit up."

Dr. Henderson smiled. "Thanks to Walt Disney, I can picture the scene rather well."

Davis was not very encouraging. "It was probably only the missus banging the dinner gong," he said. "The most infuriating part of our work is the way everything can peter out when it gets most exciting. The strata have been washed away, or there's been an earthquake—or, worse still, some silly fool has smashed up the evidence because he didn't recognize its value."

Henderson nodded in agreement. "I can sympathize with you," he said. "That's where the physicist has the advantage. He knows he'll get the answer eventually, if there is one."

He paused rather diffidently, as if weighing his words with great care. "It would save you a lot of trouble, wouldn't it, if you could actually *see* what took place in the past, without having to infer it by these laborious and uncertain methods. You've been a couple of months following these footsteps for a hundred yards, and they may lead nowhere for all your trouble."

There was a long silence. Then Barton spoke in a very thoughtful voice.

"Naturally, Doctor, we're rather curious about your work," he began. "Since Professor Fowler won't tell us anything, we've done a good deal of speculating. Do you really mean to say that——"

The physicist interrupted him rather hastily. "Don't give it any more thought," he said. "I was only daydreaming. As for our work, it's a very long way from completion, but you'll hear all about it in due course. We're not secretive—but, like everyone working in a new field, we don't want to say anything until we're sure of our ground. Why, if any other palaeontologists came near this place, I bet Professor Fowler would chase them away with a pick-axe!"

"That's not quite true," smiled Davis, "He'd be much more likely to set them to work. But I see your point of view; let's hope we don't have to wait too long."

That night, much midnight oil was burned at the main camp. Barton was frankly skeptical, but Davis had already built up an elaborate superstructure of theory around their visitor's remarks.

"It would explain so many things," he said. "First of all, their presence in this place, which otherwise doesn't make sense at all. We know the ground level here to within an inch for the last hundred million years, and we can date any event with an accuracy of better than one per cent. There's not a spot on Earth that's had its past worked out in such detail—it's the obvious place for an experiment like this!"

"But do you think it's even theoretically possible to build a machine that can see into the past?"

"I can't imagine how it could be done. But I daren't say it's impossible—especially to men like Henderson and Barnes."

"Hmmm. Not a very convincing argument. Is there any way we can hope to test it? What about those letters to *Nature?*"

"I've sent to the College Library; we should have them by the end of the week. There's always some continuity in a scientist's work, and they may give us some valuable clues."

But at first they were disappointed; indeed, Henderson's letters only increased the confusion. As Davis had remembered, most of them had been about the extraordinary properties of Helium II.

"It's really fantastic stuff," said Davis. "If a liquid behaved like this at normal temperatures, everyone would go mad. In the first place, it hasn't any viscosity at all. Sir George Darwin once said that if you had an ocean of Helium II, ships could sail in it without any engines. You'd give them a push at the beginning of their voyage and let them run into buffers on the other side. There'd be one snag, though; long before that happened the stuff would have climbed straight up the hull and the whole outfit would have sunk—gurgle, gurgle, gurgle . . ."

"Very amusing," said Barton, "but what the heck has this to do with your precious theory?"

"Not much," admitted Davis. "However, there's more to come. It's possible to have two streams of Helium II flowing in opposite directions *in the same tube*—one stream going through the other, as it were."

"That must take a bit of explaining; it's almost as bad

as an object moving in two directions at once. I suppose there *is* an explanation, something to do with Relativity, I bet."

Davis was reading carefully. "The explanation," he said slowly, "is very complicated and I don't pretend to understand it fully. But it depends on the fact that liquid helium can have *negative* entropy under certain conditions."

"As I never understood what positive entropy is, I'm not much wiser."

"Entropy is a measure of the heat distribution of the Universe. At the beginning of time, when all energy was concentrated in the suns, entropy was a minimum. It will reach its maximum when everything's at a uniform temperature and the Universe is dead. There will still be plenty of heat around, but it won't be usable."

"Whyever not?"

"Well, all the water in a perfectly flat ocean won't run a hydro-electric plant—but quite a little lake up in the hills will do the trick. You must have a difference in level."

"I get the idea. Now I come to think of it, didn't someone once call entropy 'Time's Arrow?' "

"Yes—Eddington, I believe. Any kind of clock you care to mention—a pendulum, for instance—might just as easily run forward as backward. But entropy is a strictly one-way affair—it's always increasing with the passage of time. Hence the expression, 'Time's Arrow.' "

"Then *negative* entropy—my gosh!"

For a moment the two men looked at each other. Then Barton asked in a rather subdued voice: "What does Henderson say about it?"

"I'll quote from his last letter: 'The discovery of negative entropy introduces quite new and revolutionary conceptions into our picture of the physical world. Some of these will be examined in a further communication.' "

"And are they?"

"That's the snag: there's no 'further communication.' From that you can guess two alternatives. First, the Editor of *Nature* may have declined to publish the letter. I think we can rule that one out. Second, the consequences may have been *so* revolutionary that Henderson never did write a further report."

"Negative entropy—negative time," mused Barton. "It seems fantastic; yet it might be theoretically possible to build some sort of device that could see into the past. . . ."

"I know what we'll do," said Davis suddenly. "We'll tackle the Professor about it and watch his reactions. Now I'm going to bed before I get brain fever."

That night Davis did not sleep well. He dreamed that he was walking along a road that stretched in both directions as far as the eye could see. He had been walking for miles before he came to the signpost, and when he reached it he found that it was broken and the two arms were revolving idly in the wind. As they turned, he could read the words they carried. One said simply: To the Future; the other: To the Past.

They learned nothing from Professor Fowler, which was not surprising; next to the Dean, he was the best poker player in the College. He regarded his slightly fretful assistants with no trace of emotion while Davis trotted out his theory.

When the young man had finished, he said quietly, "I'm going over again tomorrow, and I'll tell Henderson about your detective work. Maybe he'll take pity on you; maybe he'll tell me a bit more, for that matter. Now let's go to work."

Davis and Barton found it increasingly difficult to take a great deal of interest in their own work while their minds were filled with the enigma so near at hand. Nevertheless they continued conscientiously, though ever and again they paused to wonder if all their labor might not be in vain. If it were, they would be the first to rejoice. Supposing one could see into the past and watch history unfolding itself, back to the dawn of time! All the great secrets of the past would be revealed: one could watch the coming of life on the Earth, and the whole story of evolution from amoeba to man.

No; it was too good to be true. Having decided this,

they would go back to their digging and scraping for another half-hour until the thought would come: but what if it *were* true? And then the whole cycle would begin all over again.

When Professor Fowler returned from his second visit, he was a subdued and obviously shaken man. The only satisfaction his assistants could get from him was the statement that Henderson had listened to their theory and complimented them on their powers of deduction.

That was all; but in Davis's eyes it clinched the matter, though Barton was still doubtful. In the weeks that followed, he too began to waver, until at last they were both convinced that the theory was correct. For Professor Fowler was spending more and more of his time with Henderson and Barnes; so much so that they sometimes did not see him for days. He had almost lost interest in the excavations, and had delegated all responsibility to Barton, who was now able to use the big pneumatic drill to his heart's content.

They were uncovering several yards of footprints a day, and the spacing showed that the monster had now reached its utmost speed and was advancing in great leaps as if nearing its victim. In a few days they might reveal the evidence of some eon-old tragedy, preserved by a miracle and brought down the ages for the observation of man. Yet all this seemed very unimportant now; for it was clear from the Professor's hints and his general air of abstraction that the secret research was nearing its climax. He had told them as much, promising that in a very few days, if all went well, their wait would be ended. But beyond that he would say nothing.

Once or twice Henderson had paid them a visit, and they could see that he was now laboring under a considerable strain. He obviously wanted to talk about his work, but was not going to do so until the final tests had been completed. They could only admire his self-control and wish that it would break down. Davis had a distinct impression that the elusive Barnes was mainly responsible for his secrecy; he had something of a reputation for not publishing work until it had been checked and double-checked. If these experiments were as important as they believed, his caution was understandable, however infuriating.

Henderson had come over early that morning to collect the Professor, and as luck would have it, his car had broken down on the primitive road. This was unfortunate for Davis and Barton, who would have to walk to camp for lunch, since Professor Fowler was driving Henderson back in the jeep. They were quite prepared to put up with this if their wait was indeed coming to an end, as the others had more than half-hinted.

They had stood talking by the side of the jeep for some time before the two older scientists had driven away. It was a rather strained parting, for each side knew what the other was thinking. Finally Barton, as usual the most outspoken, remarked:

"Well, Doc, if this *is* Der Tag, I hope everything works properly. I'd like a photograph of a brontosaurus as a souvenir."

This sort of banter had been thrown at Henderson so often that he now took it for granted. He smiled without much mirth and replied, "I don't promise anything. It may be the biggest flop ever."

Davis moodily checked the tire pressure with the toe of his boot. It was a new set, he noticed, with an odd zigzag pattern he hadn't seen before.

"Whatever happens, we hope you'll tell us. Otherwise, we're going to break in one night and find out just what you're up to."

Henderson laughed. "You'll be a pair of geniuses if you can learn anything from our present lash-up. But, if all goes well, we may be having a little celebration by nightfall."

"What time do you expect to be back, Chief?"

"Somewhere around four. I don't want you to have to walk back for tea."

"O.K.—here's hoping!"

The machine disappeared in a cloud of dust, leaving two very thoughtful geologists standing by the roadside. Then Barton shrugged his shoulders.

"The harder we work," he said, "the quicker the time will go. Come along!"

The end of the trench, where Barton was working with the power drill, was now more than a hundred yards from the main excavation. Davis was putting the final touches to the last prints to be uncovered. They were now very deep and widely spaced, and looking along them, one could see quite clearly where the great reptile had changed its course and started, first to run, and then to hop like an enormous kangaroo. Barton wondered what it must have felt like to see such a creature bearing down upon one with the speed of an express; then he realized that if their guess was true this was exactly what they might soon be seeing.

By mid-afternoon they had uncovered a record length of track. The ground had become softer, and Barton was roaring ahead so rapidly that he had almost forgotten his other preoccupations. He had left Davis yards behind, and both men were so busy that only the pangs of hunger reminded them when it was time to finish. Davis was the first to notice that it was later than they had expected, and he walked over to speak to his friend.

"It's nearly half-past four!" he said when the noise of the drill had died away. "The Chief's late—I'll be mad if he's had tea before collecting us."

"Give him another half-hour," said Barton. "I can guess what's happened. They've blown a fuse or something and it's upset their schedule."

Davis refused to be placated. "I'll be darned annoyed if we've got to walk back to camp again. Anyway, I'm going up the hill to see if there's any sign of him."

He left Barton blasting his way through the soft rock, and climbed the low hill at the side of the old riverbed. From here one could see far down the valley, and the twin stacks of the Henderson-Barnes laboratory were clearly visible against the drab landscape. But there was no sign of the moving dust-cloud that would be following the jeep: the Professor had not yet started for home.

Davis gave a snort of disgust. There was a two-mile

walk ahead of them, after a particularly tiring day, and to make matters worse they'd now be late for tea. He decided not to wait any longer, and was already walking down the hill to rejoin Barton when something caught his eye and he stopped to look down the valley.

Around the two stacks, which were all he could see of the laboratory, a curious haze not unlike a heat tremor was playing. They must be hot, he knew, but surely not *that* hot. He looked more carefully, and saw to his amazement that the haze covered a hemisphere that must be almost a quarter of a mile across.

And, quite suddenly, it exploded. There was no light, no blinding flash; only a ripple that spread abruptly across the sky and then was gone. The haze had vanished—and so had the two great stacks of the power-house.

Feeling as though his legs had turned suddenly to water, Davis slumped down upon the hilltop and stared open-mouthed along the valley. A sense of overwhelming disaster swept into his mind; as in a dream, he waited for the explosion to reach his ears.

It was not impressive when it came; only a dull, long-drawn-out whoooooosh! that died away swiftly in the still air. Half unconsciously, Davis noticed that the chatter of the drill had also stopped; the explosion must have been louder than he thought for Barton to have heard it too.

The silence was complete. Nothing moved anywhere as far as his eye could see in the whole of that empty, barren landscape. He waited until his strength returned; then, half running, he went unsteadily down the hill to rejoin his friend.

Barton was half sitting in the trench with his head buried in his hands. He looked up as Davis approached; and although his features were obscured by dust and sand, the other was shocked at the expression in his eyes.

"So you heard it too!" Davis said. "I think the whole lab's blown up. Come along, for heaven's sake!"

"Heard what?" said Barton dully.

Davis stared at him in amazement. Then he realized that Barton could not possibly have heard any sound while he was working with the drill. The sense of disaster deepened with a rush; he felt like a character in some Greek tragedy, helpless before an implacable doom.

Barton rose to his feet. His face was working strangely, and Davis saw that he was on the verge of breakdown. Yet, when he spoke, his words were surprisingly calm.

"What fools we were!" he said. "How Henderson must have laughed at us when we told him that he was trying to *see* into the past!"

Mechanically, Davis moved to the trench and stared at the rock that was seeing the light of day for the first time in fifty million years. Without much emotion, now, he traced again the zigzag pattern he had first noticed a few hours before. It had sunk only a little way into the mud, as if when it was formed the jeep had been traveling at its utmost speed.

No doubt it had been; for in one place the shallow tire marks had been completely obliterated by the monster's footprints. They were now very deep indeed, as if the great reptile was about to make the final leap upon its desperately fleeing prey.

Jupiter Five

PROFESSOR FORSTER IS SUCH A SMALL MAN THAT A SPECIAL space-suit had to be made for him. But what he lacked in physical size he more than made up—as is so often the case—in sheer drive and determination. When I met him, he'd spent twenty years pursuing a dream. What is more to the point, he had persuaded a whole succession of hard-headed business men, World Council Delegates and administrators of scientific trusts to underwrite his expenses and to fit out a ship for him. Despite everything that happened later, I still think that was his most remarkable achievement. . . .

The "Arnold Toynbee" had a crew of six aboard when we left Earth. Besides the Professor and Charles Ashton, his chief assistant, there was the usual pilot–navigator–engineer triumvirate and two graduate students—Bill Hawkins and myself. Neither of us had ever gone into space before, and we were still so excited over the whole thing that we didn't care in the least whether we got back to Earth before the next term started. We had a strong suspicion that our tutor had very similar views. The reference he had produced for us was a masterpiece of ambiguity, but as the number of people who could even begin to read Martian script could be counted, if I may coin a phrase, on the fingers of one hand, we'd got the job.

As we were going to Jupiter, and not to Mars, the purpose of this particular qualification seemed a little obscure, though knowing something about the Professor's theories we had some pretty shrewd suspicions. They were partly confirmed when we were ten days out from Earth.

The Professor looked at us very thoughtfully when we answered his summons. Even under zero g he always managed to preserve his dignity, while the best we could do was to cling to the nearest handhold and float around like drifting seaweed. I got the impression—though I may of course be wrong—that he was thinking: What have *I* done to deserve this? as he looked from Bill to me and back again. Then he gave a sort of "It's too late to do anything about it now" sigh and began to speak in that slow, patient way he always does when he has something to explain. At least, he always uses it when he's speaking to *us*, but it's just occurred to me—oh, never mind.

"Since we left Earth," he said, "I've not had much chance of telling you the purpose of this expedition. Perhaps you've guessed it already."

"I think I have," said Bill.

"Well, go on," replied the Professor, a peculiar gleam in his eye. I did my best to stop Bill, but have you ever tried to kick anyone when you're in free fall?

"You want to find some proof—I mean, some *more* proof—of your diffusion theory of extraterrestrial culture."

"And have you any idea why I'm going to Jupiter to look for it?"

"Well, not exactly. I suppose you hope to find something on one of the moons."

"Brilliant, Bill, brilliant. There are fifteen known satellites, and their total area is about half that of Earth. Where would you start looking if you had a couple of weeks to spare? I'd rather like to know."

Bill glanced doubtfully at the Professor, as if he almost suspected him of sarcasm.

"I don't know much about astronomy," he said. "But there are four big moons, aren't there? I'd start on those."

"For your information, Io, Europa, Ganymede and Callisto are each about as big as Africa. Would you work through them in alphabetical order?"

"No," Bill replied promptly. "I'd start on the one nearest Jupiter and go outward."

"I don't think we'll waste any more time pursuing your logical processes," sighed the Professor. He was obviously impatient to begin his set speech. "Anyway, you're quite wrong. We're not going to the big moons at all. They've been photographically surveyed from space and large areas have been explored on the surface. They've got nothing of archaeological interest. *We're* going to a place that's never been visited before."

"Not to Jupiter!" I gasped.

"Heavens no, nothing as drastic as that! But we're going nearer to him than anyone else has ever been."

He paused thoughtfully.

"It's a curious thing, you know—or you probably don't —that it's nearly as difficult to travel between Jupiter's satellites as it is to go between the planets, although the distances are so much smaller. This is because Jupiter's got such a terrific gravitational field and his moons are traveling so quickly. The innermost moon's moving almost as fast as Earth, and the journey to it from Ganymede costs almost as much fuel as the trip from Earth to Venus, even though it takes only a day and a half.

"And it's *that* journey which we're going to make. No one's ever done it before because nobody could think of any good reason for the expense. Jupiter Five is only thirty kilometers in diameter, so it couldn't possibly be of much interest. Even some of the outer satellites, which are far easier to reach, haven't been visited because it hardly seemed worth while to waste the rocket fuel."

"Then why are *we* going to waste it?" I asked impatiently. The whole thing sounded like a complete wild-goose chase, though as long as it proved interesting, and involved no actual danger, I didn't greatly mind.

Perhaps I ought to confess—though I'm tempted to say nothing, as a good many others have done—that at this time I didn't believe a word of Professor Forster's theories. Of course I realized that he was a very brilliant man in his field, but I did draw the line at some of his more fantastic ideas. After all, the evidence was so slight and the conclusions so revolutionary that one could hardly help being skeptical.

Perhaps you can still remember the astonishment when the first Martian expedition found the remains not of one ancient civilization, but of two. Both had been highly advanced, but both had perished more than five million years ago. The reason was unknown (and still is). It did not seem to be warfare, as the two cultures appear to have lived amicably together. One of the races had been insect-like, the other vaguely reptilian. The insects seem to have been the genuine, original Martians. The reptile-people—usually referred to as "Culture X"—had arrived on the scene later.

So, at least, Professor Forster maintained. They had certainly possessed the secret of space travel, because the ruins of their peculiar cruciform cities had been found on —of all places—Mercury. Forster believed that they had tried to colonize all the smaller planets—Earth and Venus having been ruled out because of their excessive gravity. It was a source of some disappointment to the Professor that no traces of Culture X had ever been found on the Moon, though he was certain that such a discovery was only a matter of time.

The "conventional" theory of Culture X was that it had originally come from one of the smaller planets or satellites, had made peaceful contact with the Martians—the only other intelligent race in the known history of the System—and had died out at the same time as the Martian civilization. But Professor Forster had more ambitious ideas: he was convinced that Culture X had entered the Solar System from interstellar space. The fact that no one else believed this annoyed him, though not very much, for he is one of those people who are happy only when in a minority.

From where I was sitting, I could see Jupiter through the cabin porthole as Professor Forster unfolded his plan. It was a beautiful sight: I could just make out the equatorial cloud belts, and three of the satellites were visible as little stars close to the planet. I wondered which was Ganymede, our first port of call.

"If Jack will condescend to pay attention," the Professor continued, "I'll tell you why we're going such a long way from home. You know that last year I spent a good deal of time poking among the ruins in the twilight belt of Mercury. Perhaps you read the paper I gave on the subject at the London School of Economics. You may even have been there—I do remember a disturbance at the back of the hall.

"What I didn't tell anyone then was that while I was on Mercury I discovered an important clue to the origin of Culture X. I've kept quiet about it, although I've been sorely tempted when fools like Dr. Haughton have tried to be funny at my expense. But I wasn't going to risk letting someone else get here before I could organize this expedition.

"One of the things I found on Mercury was a rather well preserved bas-relief of the Solar System. It's not the first that's been discovered—as you know, astronomical motifs are common in true Martian and Culture X art. But there were certain peculiar symbols against various planets, including Mars and Mercury. I think the pattern had some historic significance, and the most curious thing about it is that little Jupiter Five—one of the least important of all the satellites—seemed to have the most attention drawn to it. I'm convinced that there's something on Five which is the key to the whole problem of Culture X, and I'm going there to discover what it is."

As far as I can remember now, neither Bill nor I was particularly impressed by the Professor's story. Maybe the people of Culture X had left some artifacts on Five for obscure reasons of their own. It would be interesting to unearth them, but hardly likely that they would be as important as the Professor thought. I guess he was rather disappointed at our lack of enthusiasm. If so it was his fault since, as we discovered later, he was still holding out on us.

We landed on Ganymede, the largest moon, about a week later. Ganymede is the only one of the satellites with a permanent base on it; there's an observatory and a geophysical station with a staff of about fifty scientists. They were rather glad to see visitors, but we didn't stay long as the Professor was anxious to refuel and set off again. The fact that we were heading for Five naturally aroused a good deal of interest, but the Professor wouldn't talk and we couldn't; he kept too close an eye on us.

Ganymede, by the way, is quite an interesting place and we managed to see rather more of it on the return journey. But as I've promised to write an article for another magazine about that, I'd better not say anything else here. (You might like to keep your eyes on the *National Astrographic* Magazine next Spring.)

The hop from Ganymede to Five took just over a day and a half, and it gave us an uncomfortable feeling to see Jupiter expanding hour by hour until it seemed as if he was going to fill the sky. I don't know much about astronomy, but I couldn't help thinking of the tremendous gravity field into which we were falling. All sorts of things could go wrong so easily. If we ran out of fuel we'd never be able to get back to Ganymede, and we might even drop into Jupiter himself.

I wish I could describe what it was like seeing that colossal globe, with its raging storm belts spinning in the sky ahead of us. As a matter of fact I *did* make the attempt, but some literary friends who have read this MS advised me to cut out the result. (They also gave me a lot of other advice which I don't think they could have meant seriously, because if I'd followed it there would have been no story at all.)

Luckily there have been so many color close-ups of Jupiter published by now that you're bound to have seen some of them. You may even have seen the one which, as I'll explain later, was the cause of all our trouble.

At last Jupiter stopped growing: we'd swung into the orbit of Five and would soon catch up with the tiny moon as it raced around the planet. We were all squeezed in the control room waiting for our first glimpse of our target. At least, all of us who could get in were doing so. Bill and I were crowded out into the corridor and could only crane over other people's shoulders. Kingsley Searle, our pilot, was in the control seat looking as unruffled as ever: Eric Fulton, the engineer, was thoughtfully chewing his mustache and watching the fuel gauges, and Tony Groves was doing complicated things with his navigation tables.

And the Professor appeared to be rigidly attached to the eyepiece of the teleperiscope. Suddenly he gave a start and we heard a whistle of indrawn breath. After a minute, without a word, he beckoned to Searle, who took his place at the eyepiece. Exactly the same thing happened, and then Searle handed over to Fulton. It got a bit monotonous by the time Groves had reacted identically, so we wormed our way in and took over after a bit of opposition.

I don't know quite what I'd expected to see, so that's probably why I was disappointed. Hanging there in space was a tiny gibbous moon, its "night" sector lit up faintly by the reflected glory of Jupiter. And that seemed to be all.

Then I began to make out additional markings, in the way that you do if you look through a telescope for long enough. There were faint crisscrossing lines on the surface of the satellite, and suddenly my eye grasped their full pattern. For it *was* a pattern: those lines covered Five with the same geometrical accuracy as the lines of latitude and longitude divide up a globe of the Earth. I suppose I gave my whistle of amazement, for then Bill pushed me out of the way and had his turn to look.

The next thing I remember is Professor Forster looking very smug while we bombarded him with questions.

"Of course," he explained, "this isn't as much a surprise to me as it is to you. Besides the evidence I'd found on Mercury, there were other clues. I've a friend at the Ganymede Observatory whom I've sworn to secrecy and who's been under quite a strain this last few weeks. It's rather surprising to anyone who's not an astronomer that the Observatory has never bothered much about the satellites. The big instruments are all used on extra-galactic nebulae, and the little ones spend all their time looking at Jupiter.

"The only thing the Observatory had ever done to Five was to measure its diameter and take a few photographs. They weren't quite good enough to show the markings we've just observed, otherwise there would have been an investigation before. But my friend Lawton detected them through the hundred-centimeter reflector when I asked him to look, and he also noticed something else that should have been spotted before. Five is only thirty kilometers in diameter, but it's much brighter than it should be for its size. When you compare its reflecting power—its aldeb—its——"

"Its albedo."

"Thanks, Tony—its albedo with that of the other Moons, you find that it's a much better reflector than it should be. In fact, it behaves more like polished metal than rock."

"So that explains it!" I said. "The people of Culture X must have covered Five with an outer shell—like the domes they built on Mercury, but on a bigger scale."

The Professor looked at me rather pityingly.

"So you still haven't guessed!" he said.

I don't think this was quite fair. Frankly, would you have done any better in the same circumstances?

We landed three hours later on an enormous metal plain. As I looked through the portholes, I felt completely dwarfed by my surroundings. An ant crawling on the top of an oil-storage tank might have had much the same feelings—and the looming bulk of Jupiter up there in the sky didn't help. Even the Professor's usual cockiness now seemed to be overlaid by a kind of reverent awe.

The plain wasn't quite devoid of features. Running across it in various directions were broad bands where the stupendous metal plates had been joined together. These bands, or the crisscross pattern they formed, were what we had seen from space.

About a quarter of a kilometer away was a low hill—at least, what would have been a hill on a natural world. We had spotted it on our way in after making a careful survey of the little satellite from space. It was one of six such projections, four arranged equidistantly around the equator and the other two at the Poles. The assumption was pretty obvious that they would be entrances to the world below the metal shell.

I know that some people think it must be very entertaining to walk around on an airless, low-gravity planet in spacesuits. Well, it isn't. There are so many points to think about, so many checks to make and precautions to observe, that the mental strain outweighs the glamor—at least as far as I'm concerned. But I must admit that this time, as we climbed out of the airlock, I was so excited that for once these things didn't worry me.

The gravity of Five was so microscopic that walking was completely out of the question. We were all roped together like mountaineers and blew ourselves across the metal plain with gentle bursts from our recoil pistols. The experienced astronauts, Fulton and Groves, were at the two ends of the chain so that any unwise eagerness on the part of the people in the middle was restrained.

It took us only a few minutes to reach our objective, which we discovered to be a broad, low dome at least a kilometer in circumference. I wondered if it was a gigantic airlock, large enough to permit the entrance of whole spaceships. Unless we were very lucky, we might be unable to find a way in, since the controlling mechanisms would no longer be functioning, and even if they were, we would not know how to operate them. It would be difficult to imagine anything more tantalizing than being locked out, unable to get at the greatest archaeological find in all history.

We had made a quarter circuit of the dome when we found an opening in the metal shell. It was quite small— only about two meters across—and it was so nearly circular that for a moment we did not realize what it was. Then Tony's voice came over the radio:

"That's not artificial. We've got a meteor to thank for it."

"Impossible!" protested Professor Forster. "It's much too regular."

Tony was stubborn.

"Big meteors always produce circular holes, unless they strike very glancing blows. And look at the edges; you can see there's been an explosion of some kind. Probably the meteor and the shell were vaporized; we won't find any fragments."

"You'd expect this sort of thing to happen," put in Kingsley. "How long has this been here? Five million years? I'm surprised we haven't found any other craters."

"Maybe you're right," said the Professor, too pleased to argue. "Anyway, I'm going in first."

"Right," said Kingsley, who as captain has the last say in all such matters. "I'll give you twenty meters of rope and will sit in the hole so that we can keep radio contact. Otherwise this shell will blanket your signals."

So Professor Forster was the first man to enter Five, as he deserved to be. We crowded close to Kingsley so that he could relay news of the Professor's progress.

He didn't get very far. There was another shell just inside the outer one, as we might have expected. The Professor had room to stand upright between them, and as far as his torch could throw its beam he could see avenues of supporting struts and girders, but that was about all.

It took us about twenty-four exasperating hours before we got any further. Near the end of that time I remember asking the Professor why he hadn't thought of bringing any explosives. He gave me a very hurt look.

"There's enough aboard the ship to blow us all to glory," he said. "But I'm not going to risk doing any damage if I can find another way."

That's what I call patience, but I could see his point of view. After all, what was another few days in a search that had already taken him twenty years?

It was Bill Hawkins, of all people, who found the way in when we had abandoned our first line of approach. Near the North Pole of the little world he discovered a really giant meteor hole—about a hundred meters across and cutting through both the outer shells surrounding Five. It had revealed still another shell below those, and by one of those chances that must happen if one waits enough eons, a second, smaller, meteor had come down inside the crater and penetrated the innermost skin. The hole was just big enough to allow entrance for a man in a spacesuit. We went through head first, one at a time.

I don't suppose I'll ever have a weirder experience than hanging from that tremendous vault, like a spider suspended beneath the dome of St. Peter's. We only knew that the space in which we floated was vast. Just *how* big it was we could not tell, for our torches gave us no sense of distance. In this airless, dustless cavern the beams were, of course, totally invisible and when we shone them on the roof above, we could see the ovals of light dancing away into the distance until they were too diffuse to be visible. If we pointed them "downward" we could see a pale smudge of illumination so far below that it revealed nothing.

Very slowly, under the minute gravity of this tiny world, we fell downward until checked by our safety ropes. Overhead I could see the tiny glimmering patch through which we had entered; it was remote but reassuring.

And then, while I was swinging with an infinitely sluggish pendulum motion at the end of my cable, with the lights of my companions glimmering like fitful stars in the darkness around me, the truth suddenly crashed into my brain. Forgetting that we were all on open circuit, I cried out involuntarily:

"Professor—I don't believe this is a planet at all! *It's a spaceship!*"

Then I stopped, feeling that I had made a fool of myself. There was a brief, tense silence, then a babble of noise as everyone else started arguing at once. Professor Forster's voice cut across the confusion and I could tell that he was both pleased and surprised.

"You're quite right, Jack. This is the ship that brought Culture X to the Solar System."

I heard someone—it sounded like Eric Fulton—give a gasp of incredulity.

"It's fantastic! A ship thirty kilometers across!"

"*You* ought to know better than that," replied the Professor with surprising mildness. "Suppose a civilization wanted to cross interstellar space—how else would it attack the problem? It would build a mobile planetoid out in space, taking perhaps centuries over the task. Since the ship would have to be a self-contained world, which could support its inhabitants for generations, it would need to be as large as this. I wonder how many suns they visited before they found ours and knew that their search was ended? They must have had smaller ships that could take them down to the planets, and of course they had to leave the parent vessel somewhere in space. So they parked it here, in a close orbit near the largest planet, where it would remain safely forever—or until they needed it again. It was the logical place: if they had set it circling the Sun, in time the pulls of the planets would have disturbed its orbit so much that it might have been lost. That could never happen to it here."

"Tell me, Professor," someone asked, "did you guess all this before we started?"

"I *hoped* it. All the evidence pointed to this answer. There's always been something anomalous about Satellite Five, though no one seems to have noticed it. Why this single tiny moon so close to Jupiter, when all the other small satellites are seventy times further away? Astronomically speaking, it didn't make sense. But enough of this chattering. We've got work to do."

That, I think, must count as the understatement of the century. There were seven of us faced with the greatest archaeological discovery of all time. Almost a whole world —a small world, an artificial one, but still a world—was waiting for us to explore. All we could perform was a swift and superficial reconnaissance: there might be material here for generations of research workers.

The first step was to lower a powerful floodlight on a power line running from the ship. This would act as a beacon and prevent us getting lost, as well as giving local illumination on the inner surface of the satellite. (Even now, I still find it hard to call Five a ship.) Then we dropped down the line to the surface below. It was a fall of about a kilometer, and in this low gravity it was quite safe to make the drop unretarded. The gentle shock of the impact could be absorbed easily enough by the spring-loaded staffs we carried for that purpose.

I don't want to take up any space here with yet another description of all the wonders of Satellite Five; there have already been enough pictures, maps and books on the subject. (My own, by the way is being published by Sidgwick and Jackson next Summer.) What I would like to give you instead is some impression of what it was actually *like* to be the first men ever to enter that strange metal world. Yet I'm sorry to say—I know this sounds hard to believe—I simply can't remember what I was feeling when we came across the first of the great mushroom-capped entrance shafts. I suppose I was so excited and so overwhelmed by the wonder of it all that I've forgotten everything else. But I can recall the impression of sheer size, something which mere photographs can never give. The builders of this world, coming as they did from a planet of low gravity, were giants—about four times as tall as men. We were pigmies crawling among their works.

We never got below the outer levels on our first visit, so we met few of the scientific marvels which later expeditions discovered. That was just as well; the residential areas provided enough to keep us busy for several lifetimes. The globe we were exploring must once have been lit by artificial sunlight pouring down from the triple shell that surrounded it and kept its atmosphere from leaking into space. Here on the surface the Jovians (I suppose I cannot avoid adopting the popular name for the people of Culture X) had reproduced, as accurately as they could, conditions on the world they had left unknown ages ago. Perhaps they still had day and night, changing seasons, rain and mist. They had even taken a tiny sea with them into exile. The water was still there, forming a frozen lake three kilometers across. I hear that there is a plan afoot to electrolize it and provide Five with a breathable atmosphere again, as soon as the meteor holes in the outer shell have been plugged.

The more we saw of their work, the more we grew to like the race whose possessions we were disturbing for the first time in five million years. Even if they were giants from another sun, they had much in common with man, and it is a great tragedy that our races missed each other by what is, on the cosmic scale, such a narrow margin.

We were, I suppose, more fortunate than any archaeologists in history. The vacuum of space had preserved everything from decay and—this was something which could not have been expected—the Jovians had not emptied their mighty ship of all its treasures when they had set out to colonize the Solar System. Here on the inner surface of Five everything still seemed intact, as it had been at the end of the ship's long journey. Perhaps the travelers had preserved it as a shrine in memory of their lost home, or perhaps they had thought that one day they might have to use these things again.

Whatever the reason, everything was here as its makers had left it. Sometimes it frightened me. I might be photographing, with Bill's help, some great wall carving when the sheer *timelessness* of the place would strike into my heart. I would look round nervously, half expecting to see giant shapes come stalking in through the pointed doorways, to continue the tasks that had been momentarily interrupted.

We discovered the art gallery on the fourth day. That was the only name for it; there was no mistaking its purpose. When Groves and Searle, who had been doing rapid sweeps over the southern hemisphere, reported the discovery we decided to concentrate all our forces there. For, as somebody or other has said, the art of a people reveals its soul, and here we might find the key to Culture X.

The building was huge, even by the standards of this giant race. Like all the other structures on Five, it was made of metal, yet there was nothing cold or mechanical about it. The topmost peak climbed half way to the remote roof of the world, and from a distance—before the details were visible—the building looked not unlike a Gothic cathedral. Misled by this chance resemblance, some later writers have called it a temple; but we have never found any trace of what might be called a religion among the Jovians. Yet there seems something appropriate about the name "The Temple of Art," and it's stuck so thoroughly that no one can change it now.

It has been estimated that there are between ten and twenty million individual exhibits in this single building— the harvest garnered during the whole history of a race that may have been much older than Man. And it was here that I found a small, circular room which at first sight seemed to be no more than the meeting place of six radiating corridors. I was by myself (and thus, I'm afraid, disobeying the Professor's orders) and taking what I thought would be a short-cut back to my companions. The dark walls were drifting silently past me as I glided along, the light of my torch dancing over the ceiling ahead. It was covered with deeply cut lettering, and I was so busy looking for familiar character groupings that for some time I paid no attention to the chamber's floor. Then I saw the statue and focused my beam upon it.

The moment when one first meets a great work of art has an impact that can never again be recaptured. In this case the subject matter made the effect all the more overwhelming. I was the first man ever to know what the Jovians had looked like, for here, carved with superb skill and authority, was one obviously modeled from life.

The slender, reptilian head was looking straight toward me, the sightless eyes staring into mine. Two of the hands were clasped upon the breast as if in resignation; the other two were holding an instrument whose purpose is still unknown. The long, powerful tail—which, like a kangaroo's, probably balanced the rest of the body—was stretched out along the ground, adding to the impression of rest or repose.

There was nothing human about the face or the body. There were, for example, no nostrils—only gill-like openings in the neck. Yet the figure moved me profoundly; the artist had spanned the barriers of time and culture in a way I should never have believed possible. "Not human—but humane" was the verdict Professor Forster gave. There were many things we could not have shared with the builders of this world, but all that was really important we would have felt in common.

Just as one can read emotions in the alien but familiar face of a dog or a horse, so it seemed that I knew the feelings of the being confronting me. Here was wisdom and authority—the calm, confident power that is shown, for example, in Bellini's famous portrait of the Doge Loredano. Yet there was sadness also—the sadness of a race which had made some stupendous effort, and made it in vain.

We still do not know why this single statue is the only representation the Jovians have ever made of themselves in their art. One would hardly expect to find taboos of this nature among such an advanced race; perhaps we will know the answer when we have deciphered the writing carved on the chamber walls.

Yet I am already certain of the statue's purpose. It was set here to bridge time and to greet whatever beings might one day stand in the footsteps of its makers. That, perhaps, is why they shaped it so much smaller than life. Even then they must have guessed that the future belonged to Earth or Venus, and hence to beings whom they would have dwarfed. They knew that size could be a barrier as well as time.

A few minutes later I was on my way back to the ship with my companions, eager to tell the Professor about the discovery. He had been reluctantly snatching some rest, though I don't believe he averaged more than four hours sleep a day all the time we were on Five. The golden light of Jupiter was flooding the great metal plain as we emerged through the shell and stood beneath the stars once more.

"Hello!" I heard Bill say over the radio, "the Prof's moved the ship."

"Nonsense," I retorted. "It's exactly where we left it."

Then I turned my head and saw the reason for Bill's mistake. We had visitors.

The second ship had come down a couple of kilometers away, and as far as my non-expert eyes could tell it might have been a duplicate of ours. When we hurried through the airlock, we found that the Professor, a little bleary-eyed, was already entertaining. To our surprise, though not exactly to our displeasure, one of the three visitors was an extremely attractive brunette.

"This," said Professor Forster, a little wearily, "is Mr. Randolph Mays, the science writer. I imagine you've heard of him. And this is——" He turned to Mays. "I'm afraid I didn't quite catch the names."

"My pilot, Donald Hopkins—my secretary, Marianne Mitchell."

There was just the slightest pause before the word "secretary," but it was long enough to set a little signal light flashing in my brain. I kept my eyebrows from going up, but I caught a glance from Bill that said, without any need for words: If you're thinking what I'm thinking, I'm ashamed of you.

Mays was a tall, rather cadaverous man with thinning hair and an attitude of bonhomie which one felt was only skin-deep—the protective coloration of a man who has to be friendly with too many people.

"I expect this is as big a surprise to you as it is to me," he said with unnecessary heartiness. "I certainly never expected to find anyone here before me; and I certainly didn't expect to find all *this*."

"What brought you here?" said Ashton, trying to sound not too suspiciously inquisitive.

"I was just explaining that to the Professor. Can I have that folder please, Marianne? Thanks."

He drew out a series of very fine astronomical paintings and passed them round. They showed the planets from their satellites—a common-enough subject, of course.

"You've all seen this sort of thing before," Mays continued. "But there's a difference here. These pictures are nearly a hundred years old. They were painted by an artist named Chesley Bonestell and appeared in *Life* back in 1944—long before space-travel began, of course. Now what's happened is that *Life* has commissioned me to go round the Solar System and see how well I can match these imaginative paintings against the reality. In the centenary issue, they'll be published side by side with photographs of the real thing. Good idea, eh?"

I had to admit that it was. But it was going to make matters rather complicated, and I wondered what the Professor thought about it. Then I glanced again at Miss Mitchell, standing demurely in the corner, and decided that there would be compensations.

In any other circumstances, we would have been glad to meet another party of explorers, but here there was the question of priority to be considered. Mays would certainly be hurrying back to Earth as quickly as he could, his original mission abandoned and all his film used up here and now. It was difficult to see how we could stop him, and not even certain that we desired to do so. We wanted all the publicity and support we could get, but we would prefer to do things in our own time, after our own fashion. I wondered how strong the Professor was on tact, and feared the worst.

Yet at first diplomatic relations were smooth enough. The Professor had hit upon the bright idea of pairing each of us with one of Mays's team, so that we acted simultaneously as guides and supervisors. Doubling the number of investigating groups also greatly increased the rate at which we could work. It was unsafe for anyone to operate by himself under these conditions, and this had handicapped us a great deal.

The Professor outlined his policy to us the day after the arrival of Mays's party.

"I hope we can get along together," he said a little anxiously. "As far as I'm concerned they can go where they like and photograph what they like, as long as *they don't take anything*, and as long as they don't get back to Earth with their records before we do."

"I don't see how we can stop them," protested Ashton.

"Well, I hadn't intended to do this, but I've now registered a claim to Five. I radioed it to Ganymede last night, and it will be at The Hague by now."

"But no one can claim an astronomical body for himself. That was settled in the case of the Moon, back in the last century."

The Professor gave a rather crooked smile.

"I'm not annexing an *astronomical body*, remember. I've put in a claim for salvage, and I've done it in the name of the World Science Organization. If Mays takes anything out of Five, he'll be stealing it from them. Tomorrow I'm going to explain the situation gently to him, just in case he gets any bright ideas."

It certainly seemed peculiar to think of Satellite Five as salvage, and I could imagine some pretty legal quarrels developing when we got home. But for the present the Professor's move should have given us some safeguards and might discourage Mays from collecting souvenirs—so we were optimistic enough to hope.

It took rather a lot of organizing, but I managed to get paired off with Marianne for several trips round the interior of Five. Mays didn't seem to mind: there was no particular reason why he should. A spacesuit is the most perfect chaperon ever devised, confound it.

Naturally enough I took her to the art gallery at the first opportunity, and showed her my find. She stood looking at the statue for a long time while I held my torch beam upon it.

"It's very wonderful," she breathed at last. "Just think of it waiting here in the darkness all those millions of years! But you'll have to give it a name."

"I have. I've christened it 'The Ambassador.'"

"Why?"

"Well, because I think it's a kind of envoy, if you like, carrying a greeting to us. The people who made it knew that one day someone else was bound to come here and find this place."

"I think you're right. 'The Ambassador'—yes, that was clever of you. There's something noble about it, and something very sad, too. Don't you feel it?"

I could tell that Marianne was a very intelligent woman. It was quite remarkable the way she saw my point of view, and the interest she took in everything I showed her. But "The Ambassador" fascinated her most of all, and she kept on coming back to it.

"You know, Jack," she said (I think this was sometime the next day, when Mays had been to see it as well) "you must take that statue back to Earth. Think of the sensation it would cause."

I sighed.

"The Professor would like to, but it must weigh a ton. We can't afford the fuel. It will have to wait for a later trip."

She looked puzzled.

"But things hardly weigh anything here," she protested.

"That's different," I explained. "There's weight, and there's inertia—two quite different things. Now inertia—

oh, never mind. We can't take it back, anyway. Captain Searle's told us that, definitely."

"What a pity," said Marianne.

I forgot all about this conversation until the night before we left. We had had a busy and exhausting day packing our equipment (a good deal, of course, we left behind for future use.) All our photographic material had been used up. As Charlie Ashton remarked, if we met a *live* Jovian now we'd be unable to record the fact. I think we were all wanting a breathing space, an opportunity to relax and sort out our impressions and to recover from our head-on collision with an alien culture.

Mays's ship, the "Henry Luce," was also nearly ready for take-off. We would leave at the same time, an arrangement which suited the Professor admirably as he did not trust Mays alone on Five.

Everything had been settled when, while checking through our records, I suddenly found that six rolls of exposed film were missing. They were photographs of a complete set of transcriptions in the Temple of Art. After a certain amount of thought I recalled that they had been entrusted to my charge, and I had put them very carefully on a ledge in the Temple, intending to collect them later.

It was a long time before take-off, the Professor and Ashton were canceling some arrears of sleep, and there seemed no reason why I should not slip back to collect the missing material. I knew there would be a row if it was left behind, and as I remembered exactly where it was I need be gone only thirty minutes. So I went, explaining my mission to Bill just in case of accidents.

The floodlight was no longer working, of course, and the darkness inside the shell of Five was somewhat oppressive. But I left a portable beacon at the entrance, and dropped freely until my hand torch told me it was time to break the fall. Ten minutes later, with a sigh of relief, I gathered up the missing films.

It was a natural-enough thing to pay my last respects to The Ambassador: it might be years before I saw him again, and that calmly enigmatic figure had begun to exercise an extraordinary fascination over me.

Unfortunately, that fascination had not been confined to me alone. For the chamber was empty and the statue gone.

I suppose I could have crept back and said nothing, thus avoiding awkward explanations. But I was too furious to think of discretion, and as soon as I returned we woke the Professor and told him what had happened.

He sat on his bunk rubbing the sleep out of his eyes, then uttered a few harsh words about Mr. Mays and his companions which it would do no good at all to repeat here.

"What I don't understand," said Searle "is how they got the thing out—if they have, in fact. We should have spotted it."

"There are plenty of hiding places, and they could have waited until there was no one around before they took it up through the hull. It must have been quite a job, even under this gravity," remarked Eric Fulton, in tones of admiration.

"There's no time for post-mortems," said the Professor savagely. "We've got five hours to think of something. They can't take off before then, because we're only just past opposition with Ganymede. That's correct, isn't it Kingsley?"

Searle nodded agreement.

"Yes. We must move round to the other side of Jupiter before we can enter a transfer orbit—at least, a reasonably economical one."

"Good. That gives us a breathing space. Well, has anyone any ideas?"

Looking back on the whole thing now, it often seems to me that our subsequent behavior was, shall I say, a little peculiar and slightly uncivilized. It was not the sort of thing we could have imagined ourselves doing a few months before. But we were annoyed and overwrought, and our remoteness from all other human beings somehow made everything seem different. Since there were no other laws here, we had to make our own. . . .

"Can't we do something to stop them from taking off?

Could we sabotage their rockets, for instance?" asked Bill.

Searle didn't like this idea at all.

"We mustn't do anything drastic," he said. "Besides, Don Hopkins is a good friend of mine. He'd never forgive me if I damaged his ship. There'd be the danger, too, that we might do something that couldn't be repaired."

"Then pinch their fuel," said Groves laconically.

"Of course! They're probably all asleep, there's no light in the cabin. All we've got to do is to connect up and pump."

"A very nice idea," I pointed out "but we're two kilometers apart. How much pipeline have we got? Is it as much as a hundred meters?"

The others ignored this interruption as though it was beneath contempt and went on making their plans. Five minutes later the technicians had settled everything: we only had to climb into our spacesuits and do the work.

I never thought, when I joined the Professor's expedition, that I should end up like an African porter in one of those old adventure stories, carrying a load on my head. Especially when that load was a sixth of a spaceship (being so short, Professor Forster wasn't able to provide very effective help). Now that its fuel tanks were half empty, the weight of the ship in this gravity was about two hundred kilograms. We squeezed beneath, heaved, and up she went—very slowly, of course, because her inertia was still unchanged. Then we started marching.

It took us quite a while to make the journey, and it wasn't quite as easy as we'd thought it would be. But presently the two ships were lying side by side, and nobody had noticed us. Everyone in the "Henry Luce" was fast asleep, as they had every reason to expect us to be.

Though I was still rather short of breath, I found a certain schoolboy amusement in the whole adventure as Searle and Fulton drew the refueling pipeline out of our airlock and quietly coupled up to the other ship.

"The beauty of this plan," explained Groves to me as we stood watching, "is that they can't do anything to stop us, unless they come outside and uncouple our line. We can drain them dry in five minutes, and it will take them half that time to wake up and get into their spacesuits."

A sudden horrid fear smote me.

"Suppose they turned on their rockets and tried to get away?"

"Then we'd both be smashed up. No, they'll just have to come outside and see what's going on. Ah, there go the pumps."

The pipeline had stiffened like a fire-hose under pressure, and I knew that the fuel was pouring into our tanks. Any moment now the lights would go on in the "Henry Luce" and her startled occupants would come scuttling out.

It was something of an anticlimax when they didn't. They must have been sleeping very soundly not to have felt the vibration from the pumps, but when it was all over nothing had happened and we just stood round looking rather foolish. Searle and Fulton carefully uncoupled the pipeline and put it back into the airlock.

"Well?" we asked the Professor.

He thought things over for a minute.

"Let's get back into the ship," he said.

When we had climbed out of our suits and were gathered together in the control room, or as far in as we could get, the Professor sat down at the radio and punched out the "Emergency" signal. Our sleeping neighbors would be awake in a couple of seconds as their automatic receiver sounded the alarm.

The TV screen glimmered into life. There, looking rather frightened, was Randolph Mays.

"Hello, Forster," he snapped. "What's the trouble?"

"Nothing wrong here," replied the Professor in his best deadpan manner, "but you've lost something important. Look at your fuel gauges."

The screen emptied, and for a moment there was a confused mumbling and shouting from the speaker. Then Mays was back, annoyance and alarm competing for possession of his features.

"What's going on?" he demanded angrily. "Do you know anything about this?"

The Prof. let him sizzle for a moment before he replied.

"I think you'd better come across and talk things over," he said. "You won't have far to walk."

Mays glared back at him uncertainly, then retorted "You bet I will!" The screen went blank.

"He'll have to climb down now!" said Bill gleefully. "There's nothing else he can do!"

"It's not so simple as you think," warned Fulton. "If he really wanted to be awkward, he could just sit tight and radio Ganymede for a tanker."

"What good would that do him? It would waste days and cost a fortune."

"Yes, but he'd still have the statue, if he wanted it that badly. And he'd get his money back when he sued us."

The airlock light flashed on and Mays stumped into the room. He was in a surprisingly conciliatory mood; on the way over, he must have had second thoughts.

"Well, well," he said affably. "What's all this nonsense in aid of?"

"You know perfectly well," the Professor retorted coldly. "I made it quite clear that nothing was to be taken off Five. You've been stealing property that doesn't belong to you."

"Now, let's be reasonable. Who *does* it belong to? You can't claim everything on this planet as your personal property."

"This is *not* a planet—it's a ship and the laws of salvage operate."

"Frankly, that's a very debatable point. Don't you think you should wait until you get a ruling from the lawyers?"

The Professor was being icily polite, but I could see that the strain was terrific and an explosion might occur at any moment.

"Listen, Mr. Mays," he said with ominous calm. "What you've taken is the most important single find we've made here. I will make allowances for the fact that you don't appreciate what you've done, and don't understand the viewpoint of an archaeologist like myself. Return that statue, and we'll pump your fuel back and say no more."

Mays rubbed his chin thoughtfully.

"I really don't see why you should make such a fuss about one statue, when you consider all the stuff that's still here."

It was then that the Professor made one of his rare mistakes.

"You talk like a man who's stolen the Mona Lisa from the Louvre and argues that nobody will miss it because of all the other paintings. This statue's unique in a way that no terrestrial work of art can ever be. That's why I'm determined to get it back."

You should never, when you're bargaining, make it obvious that you want something really badly. I saw the greedy glint in Mays's eye and said to myself "Uh-huh! He's going to be tough." And I remembered Fulton's remark about calling Ganymede for a tanker.

"Give me half an hour to think it over," said Mays, turning to the airlock.

"Very well," replied the Professor stiffly. "Half an hour —no more."

I must give Mays credit for brains. Within five minutes we saw his communications aerial start slewing round until it locked on Ganymede. Naturally we tried to listen in, but he had a scrambler. These newspaper men must trust each other.

The reply came back a few minutes later; that was scrambled, too. While we were waiting for the next development, we had another council of war. The Professor was now entering the stubborn, stop-at-nothing stage. He realized he'd miscalculated and that had made him fighting mad.

I think Mays must have been a little apprehensive, because he had reinforcements when he returned. Donald Hopkins, his pilot, came with him, looking rather uncomfortable.

"I've been able to fix things up, Professor," he said smugly. "It will take me a little longer, but I can get back without your help if I have to. Still, I must admit that it will save a good deal of time and money if we can come to an agreement. I'll tell you what. Give me back my fuel and I'll return the other—er—souvenirs I've collected. But I insist on keeping Mona Lisa, even if it means I won't get back to Ganymede until the middle of next week."

The Professor then uttered a number of what are usually called deep-space oaths, though I can assure you they're much the same as any other oaths. That seemed to relieve his feelings a lot and he became fiendishly friendly.

"My dear Mr. Mays," he said, "You're an unmitigated crook, and accordingly I've no compunction left in dealing with you. I'm prepared to use force, knowing that the law will justify me."

Mays looked slightly alarmed, though not unduly so. We had moved to strategic positions round the door.

"Please don't be so melodramatic," he said haughtily. "This is the twenty-first century, not the Wild West back in 1800."

"1880," said Bill, who is a stickler for accuracy.

"I must ask you," the Professor continued, "to consider yourself under detention while we decide what is to be done. Mr. Searle, take him to Cabin B."

Mays sidled along the wall with a nervous laugh.

"Really, Professor, this is *too* childish! You can't detain me against my will." He glanced for support at the Captain of the "Henry Luce."

Donald Hopkins dusted an imaginary speck of fluff from his uniform.

"I refuse," he remarked for the benefit of all concerned, "to get involved in vulgar brawls."

Mays gave him a venomous look and capitulated with bad grace. We saw that he had a good supply of reading matter, and locked him in.

When he was out of the way, the Professor turned to Hopkins, who was looking enviously at our fuel gauges.

"Can I take it, Captain," he said politely, "that you don't wish to get mixed up in any of your employer's dirty business?"

"I'm neutral. My job is to fly the ship here and take her home. You can fight this out among yourselves."

"Thank you. I think we understand each other perfectly. Perhaps it would be best if you returned to your ship and explained the situation. We'll be calling you in a few minutes."

Captain Hopkins made his way languidly to the door. As he was about to leave he turned to Searle.

"By the way, Kingsley," he drawled. "Have you thought of torture? Do call me if you get round to it— I've some jolly interesting ideas." Then he was gone, leaving us with our hostage.

I think the Professor had hoped he could do a direct exchange. If so, he had not bargained on Marianne's stubbornness.

"It serves Randolph right," she said. "But I don't really see that it makes any difference. He'll be just as comfortable in your ship as in ours, and you can't do anything to him. Let me know when you're fed up with having him around."

It seemed a complete impasse. We had been too clever by half, and it had got us exactly nowhere. We'd captured Mays, but he wasn't any use to us.

The Professor was standing with his back to us, staring morosely out of the window. Seemingly balanced on the horizon, the immense bulk of Jupiter nearly filled the sky.

"We've got to convince her that we really *do* mean business," he said. Then he turned abruptly to me.

"Do you think she's actually fond of this blackguard?"

"Er—I shouldn't be surprised. Yes, I really believe so."

The Professor looked very thoughtful. Then he said to Searle, "Come into my room. I want to talk something over."

They were gone quite a while. When they returned, they both had an indefinable air of gleeful anticipation, and the Professor was carrying a piece of paper covered with figures. He went to the radio, and called the "Henry Luce."

"Hello," said Marianne, replying so promptly that she'd obviously been waiting for us. "Have you decided to call it off? I'm getting so bored."

The Professor looked at her gravely.

"Miss Mitchell," he replied. "It's apparent that you have not been taking us seriously. I'm therefore arranging a somewhat—er—drastic little demonstration for your benefit. I'm going to place your employer in a position from which he'll be only too anxious for you to retrieve him as quickly as possible."

"Indeed?" replied Marianne noncommittally—though I thought I could detect a trace of apprehension in her voice.

"I don't suppose," continued the Professor smoothly, "that you know anything about celestial mechanics. No? Too bad, but your pilot will confirm everything I tell you. Won't you, Hopkins?"

"Go ahead," came a painstakingly neutral voice from the background.

"Then listen carefully, Miss Mitchell. I want to remind you of our curious—indeed our precarious—position on this satellite. You've only got to look out of the window to see how close to Jupiter we are, and I need hardly remind you that Jupiter has by far the most intense gravitational field of all the planets. You follow me?"

"Yes," replied Marianne, no longer quite so self-possessed. "Go on."

"Very well. This little world of ours goes round Jupiter in almost exactly twelve hours. Now there's a well-known theorem stating that if a body *falls* from an orbit to the center of attraction, it will take point one seven seven of a period to make the drop. In other words, anything falling from here to Jupiter would reach the center of the planet in about two hours seven minutes. I'm sure Captain Hopkins can confirm this."

There was a long pause. Then we heard Hopkins say, "Well, of course I can't confirm the exact figures, but they're probably correct. It would be something like that, anyway."

"Good," continued the Professor. "Now I'm sure you realize," he went on with a hearty chuckle, "that a fall to the *center* of the planet is a very theoretical case. If anything really was dropped from here, it would reach the upper atmosphere of Jupiter in a considerably shorter time. I hope I'm not boring you?"

"No," said Marianne, rather faintly.

"I'm so glad to hear it. Anyway, Captain Searle has worked out the actual time for me, and it's one hour thirty five minutes—with a few minutes either way. We can't guarantee complete accuracy, ha, ha!"

"Now, it has doubtless not escaped your notice that this satellite of ours has an extremely weak gravitational field. It's escape velocity is only about ten meters a second, and anything thrown away from it at that speed would never come back. Correct, Mr. Hopkins?"

"Perfectly correct."

"Then, if I may come to the point, we propose to take Mr. Mays for a walk until he's immediately under Jupiter, remove the reaction pistols from his suit, and—ah—launch him forth. We will be prepared to retrieve him with our ship as soon as you've handed over the property you've stolen. After what I've told you, I'm sure you'll appreciate that time will be rather vital. An hour and thirty five minutes is remarkably short, isn't it?"

"Professor!" I gasped, "You can't possibly do this!"

"Shut up!" he barked. "Well, Miss Mitchell, what about it?"

Marianne was staring at him with mingled horror and disbelief.

"You're simply bluffing!" she cried. "I don't believe you'd do anything of the kind! Your crew won't let you!"

The Professor sighed.

"Too bad," he said. "Captain Searle—Mr. Groves—will you take the prisoner and proceed as instructed."

"Aye-aye, sir," replied Searle with great solemnity.

Mays looked frightened but stubborn.

"What are you going to do now?" he said, as his suit was handed back to him.

Searle unholstered his reaction pistols. "Just climb in," he said. "We're going for a walk."

I realized then what the Professor hoped to do. The whole thing was a colossal bluff: of course he wouldn't *really* have Mays thrown into Jupiter; and in any case Searle and Groves wouldn't do it. Yet surely Marianne would see through the bluff, and then we'd be left looking mighty foolish.

Mays couldn't run away; without his reaction pistols he was quite helpless. Grasping his arms and towing him along like a captive balloon, his escorts set off toward the horizon—and towards Jupiter.

I could see, looking across the space to the other ship, that Marianne was staring out through the observation windows at the departing trio. Professor Forster noticed it too.

"I hope you're convinced, Miss Mitchell, that my men aren't carrying along an empty spacesuit. Might I suggest that you follow the proceedings with a telescope? They'll be over the horizon in a minute, but you'll be able to see Mr. Mays when he starts to—er—ascend."

There was a stubborn silence from the loudspeaker. The period of suspense seemed to last for a very long time. Was Marianne waiting to see how far the Professor really would go?

By this time I had got hold of a pair of binoculars and was sweeping the sky beyond the ridiculously close horizon. Suddenly I saw it—a tiny flare of light against the vast yellow back-cloth of Jupiter. I focused quickly, and could just make out the three figures rising into space. As I watched, they separated: two of them decelerated with their pistols and started to fall back toward Five. The other went on ascending helplessly toward the ominous bulk of Jupiter.

I turned on the Professor in horror and disbelief.

"They've really done it!" I cried. "I thought you were only bluffing!"

"So did Miss Mitchell, I've no doubt," said the Professor calmly, for the benefit of the listening microphone. "I hope I don't need to impress upon you the urgency of the situation. As I've remarked once or twice before, the time of fall from our orbit to Jupiter's surface is ninety-five minutes. But, of course, if one waited even half that time, it would be much too late. . . ."

He let that sink in. There was no reply from the other ship.

"And now," he continued, "I'm going to switch off our receiver so we can't have any more arguments. We'll wait until you've unloaded that statue—*and* the other items Mr. Mays was careless enough to mention—before we'll talk to you again. Good-by."

It was a very uncomfortable ten minutes. I'd lost track of Mays, and was seriously wondering if we'd better overpower the Professor and go after him before we had a murder on our hands. But the people who could fly the ship were the ones who had actually carried out the crime. I didn't know *what* to think.

Then the airlock of the "Henry Luce" slowly opened. A couple of space-suited figures emerged, floating the cause of all the trouble between them.

"Unconditional surrender," murmured the Professor with a sigh of satisfaction. "Get it into our ship," he called over the radio, "I'll open up the airlock for you."

He seemed in no hurry at all. I kept looking anxiously at the clock; fifteen minutes had already gone by. Presently there was a clanking and banging in the airlock, the inner door opened, and Captain Hopkins entered. He was followed by Marianne, who only needed a bloodstained axe to make her look like Clytaemnestra. I did my best to avoid her eye, but the Professor seemed to be quite without shame. He walked into the airlock, checked that his property was back, and emerged rubbing his hands.

"Well, that's that," he said cheerfully. "Now let's sit down and have a drink to forget all this unpleasantness, shall we?"

I pointed indignantly at the clock.

"Have you gone crazy!" I yelled. "He's already halfway to Jupiter!"

Professor Forster looked at me disapprovingly.

"Impatience," he said, "is a common failing in the young. I see no cause at all for hasty action."

Marianne spoke for the first time; she now looked really scared.

"But you promised," she whispered.

The Professor suddenly capitulated. He had had his little joke, and didn't want to prolong the agony.

"I can tell you at once, Miss Mitchell—and you too, Jack—that Mays is in no more danger than we are. We can go and collect him whenever we like."

"Do you mean that you lied to me?"

"Certainly not. Everything I told you was perfectly true. You simply jumped to the wrong conclusions. When I said that a body would take ninety-five minutes to fall from here to Jupiter, I omitted—not, I must confess, accidentally—a rather important phrase. I should have added *"a body at rest with respect to Jupiter."* Your friend Mr. Mays was sharing the orbital speed of this satellite, and he's still got it. A little matter of twenty-six kilometers a second, Miss Mitchell.

"Oh yes, we threw him completely off Five and toward Jupiter. But the velocity we gave him then was trivial. He's still moving in practically the same orbit as before. The most he can do—I've got Captain Searle to work out the figures—is to drift about a hundred kilometers inward. And in one revolution—twelve hours—*he'll be right back where he started*, without us bothering to do anything at all."

There was a long, long silence. Marianne's face was a study in frustration, relief, and annoyance at having been fooled. Then she turned on Captain Hopkins.

"You must have known all the time! Why didn't you tell me?"

Hopkins gave her a wounded expression.

"You didn't ask me," he said.

We hauled Mays down about an hour later. He was only twenty kilometers up, and we located him quickly enough by the flashing light on his suit. His radio had been disconnected, for a reason that hadn't occurred to me. He was intelligent enough to realize that he was in no danger, and if his set had been working he could have called his ship and exposed our bluff. That is, if he wanted to. Personally, I think I'd have been glad enough to call the whole thing off even if I had known that I was perfectly safe. It must have been awfully lonely up there.

To my great surprise, Mays wasn't as mad as I'd expected. Perhaps he was too relieved to be back in our snug little cabin when we drifted up to him on the merest fizzle of rockets and yanked him in. Or perhaps he felt that he'd been worsted in fair fight and didn't bear any grudge. I really think it was the latter.

There isn't much more to tell, except that we did play one other trick on him before we left Five. He had a good deal more fuel in his tanks than he really needed, now that his payload was substantially reduced. By keeping the excess ourselves, we were able to carry The Ambassador back to Ganymede after all. Oh, yes, the Professor gave him a cheque for the fuel we'd borrowed. Everything was perfectly legal.

There's one amusing sequel I must tell you, though. The day after the new gallery was opened at the British Museum I went along to see The Ambassador, partly to discover if his impact was still as great in these changed surroundings. (For the record, it wasn't—though it's still considerable and Bloomsbury will never be quite the same to me again.) A huge crowd was milling around the gallery, and there in the middle of it was Mays and Marianne.

It ended up with us having a very pleasant lunch together in Holborn. I'll say this about Mays—he doesn't bear any grudges. But I'm still rather sore about Marianne.

And, frankly, I can't imagine *what* she sees in him.

The Possessed

AND NOW THE SUN AHEAD WAS SO CLOSE THAT THE HURRI-cane of radiation was forcing the Swarm back into the dark night of space. Soon it would be able to come no closer; the gales of light on which it rode from star to star could not be faced so near their source. Unless it encountered a planet very soon, and could fall down into the peace and safety of its shadow, this sun must be abandoned as had so many before.

Six cold outer worlds had already been searched and discarded. Either they were frozen beyond all hope of organic life, or else they harbored entities of types that were useless to the Swarm. If it was to survive, it must find hosts not too unlike those it had left on its doomed and distant home. Millions of years ago the Swarm had begun its journey, swept starward by the fires of its own exploding sun. Yet even now the memory of its lost birthplace was still sharp and clear, an ache that would never die.

There was a planet ahead, swinging its cone of shadow through the flame-swept night. The senses that the Swarm had developed upon its long journey reached out toward the approaching world, reached out and found it good.

The merciless buffeting of radiation ceased as the black disc of the planet eclipsed the sun. Falling freely under gravity, the Swarm dropped swiftly until it hit the outer fringe of the atmosphere. The first time it had made planetfall it had almost met its doom, but now it contracted its tenuous substance with the unthinking skill of long practice, until it formed a tiny, close-knit sphere. Slowly its velocity slackened, until at last it was floating motionless between earth and sky.

For many years it rode the winds of the stratosphere

from Pole to Pole, or let the soundless fusillades of dawn blast it westward from the rising sun. Everywhere it found life, but nowhere intelligence. There were things that crawled and flew and leaped, but there were no things that talked or built. Ten million years hence there might be creatures here with minds that the Swarm could possess and guide for its own purposes; there was no sign of them now. It could not guess which of the countless life-forms on this planet would be the heir to the future, and without such a host it was helpless—a mere pattern of electric charges, a matrix of order and self-awareness in a universe of chaos. By its own resources the Swarm had no control over matter, yet once it had lodged in the mind of a sentient race there was nothing that lay beyond its powers.

It was not the first time, and it would not be the last, that the planet had been surveyed by a visitant from space —though never by one in such peculiar and urgent need. The Swarm was faced with a tormenting dilemma. It could begin its weary travels once more, hoping that ultimately it might find the conditions it sought, or it could wait here on this world, biding its time until a race had arisen which would fit its purpose.

It moved like mist through the shadows, letting the vagrant winds take it where they willed. The clumsy, ill-formed reptiles of this young world never saw its passing, but it observed them, recording, analyzing, trying to extrapolate into the future. There was so little to choose between all these creatures; not one showed even the first faint glimmerings of conscious mind. Yet if it left this world in search of another, it might roam the universe in vain until the end of time.

At last it made its decision. By its very nature, it could choose both alternatives. The greater part of the Swarm would continue its travels among the stars, but a portion of it would remain on this world, like a seed planted in the hope of future harvest.

It began to spin upon its axis, its tenuous body flattening into a disc. Now it was wavering at the frontiers of visibility—it was a pale ghost, a faint will-of-the-wisp that suddenly fissured into two unequal fragments. The spinning slowly died away: the Swarm had become two, each an entity with all the memories of the original, and all its desires and needs.

There was a last exchange of thoughts between parent and child who were also identical twins. If all went well with them both, they would meet again in the far future here at this valley in the mountains. The one who was staying would return to this point at regular intervals down the ages; the one who continued the search would send back an emissary if ever a better world was found. And then they would be united again, no longer homeless exiles vainly wandering among the indifferent stars.

The light of dawn was spilling over the raw, new mountains when the parent swarm rose up to meet the sun. At the edge of the atmosphere the gales of radiation caught it and swept it unresisting out beyond the planets, to start again upon the endless search.

The one that was left began its almost equally hopeless task. It needed an animal that was not so rare that disease or accident could make it extinct, nor so tiny that it could never acquire any power over the physical world. And it must breed rapidly, so that its evolution could be directed and controlled as swiftly as possible.

The search was long and the choice difficult, but at last the Swarm selected its host. Like rain sinking into thirsty soil, it entered the bodies of certain small lizards and began to direct their destiny.

It was an immense task, even for a being which could never know death. Generation after generation of the lizards was swept into the past before there came the slightest improvement in the race. And always, at the appointed time, the Swarm returned to its rendezvous among the mountains. Always it returned in vain: there was no messenger from the stars, bringing news of better fortune elsewhere.

The centuries lengthened into millennia, the millennia into eons. By the standards of geological time, the lizards were now changing rapidly. Presently they were lizards no more, but warm-blooded, fur-covered creatures that brought forth their young alive. They were still small and feeble, and their minds were rudimentary, but they contained the seeds of future greatness.

Yet not only the living creatures were altering as the ages slowly passed. Continents were being rent asunder, mountains being worn down by the weight of the unwearying rain. Through all these changes, the Swarm kept to its purpose; and always, at the appointed times, it went to the meeting place that had been chosen so long ago, waited patiently for a while, and came away. Perhaps the parent swarm was still searching or perhaps—it was a hard and terrible thought to grasp—some unknown fate had overtaken it and it had gone the way of the race it had once ruled. There was nothing to do but to wait and see if the stubborn life-stuff of this planet could be forced along the path to intelligence.

And so the eons passed. . . .

Somewhere in the labyrinth of evolution the Swarm made its fatal mistake and took the wrong turning. A hundred million years had gone since it came to Earth, and it was very weary. It could not die, but it could degenerate. The memories of its ancient home and of its destiny were fading: its intelligence was waning even while its hosts climbed the long slope that would lead to self-awareness.

By a cosmic irony, in giving the impetus which would one day bring intelligence to this world, the Swarm had exhausted itself. It had reached the last stage of parasitism; no longer could it exist apart from its hosts. Never again could it ride free above the world, driven by wind and sun. To make the pilgrimage to the ancient rendezvous, it must travel slowly and painfully in a thousand little bodies. Yet it continued the immemorial custom, driven on by the desire for reunion which burned all the more fiercely now that it knew the bitterness of failure. Only if the parent swarm returned and reabsorbed it could it ever know new life and vigor.

The glaciers came and went; by a miracle the little beasts that now housed the waning alien intelligence escaped the clutching fingers of the ice. The oceans overwhelmed the land, and still the race survived. It even multiplied, but it could do no more. This world would never be its heritage, for far away in the heart of another continent a certain monkey had come down from the trees and was looking at the stars with the first glimmerings of curiosity.

The mind of the Swarm was dispersing, scattering among a million tiny bodies, no longer able to unite and assert its will. It had lost all cohesion; its memories were fading. In a million years, at most, they would all be gone.

Only one thing remained—the blind urge which still, at intervals which by some strange aberration were becoming ever shorter, drove it to seek its consummation in a valley that long ago had ceased to exist.

Quietly riding the lane of moonlight, the pleasure steamer passed the island with its winking beacon and entered the fjord. It was a calm and lovely night, with Venus sinking in the west out beyond the Faroes, and the lights of the harbor reflected with scarcely a tremor in the still waters far ahead.

Nils and Christina were utterly content. Standing side by side against the boat rail, their fingers locked together, they watched the wooded slopes drift silently by. The tall trees were motionless in the moonlight, their leaves unruffled by even the merest breath of wind, their slender trunks rising whitely from pools of shadow. The whole world was asleep; only the moving ship dared to break the spell that had bewitched the night.

Then suddenly, Christina gave a little gasp and Nils felt her fingers tighten convulsively on his. He followed her gaze: she was staring out across the water, looking toward the silent sentinels of the forest.

"What is it, darling?" he asked anxiously.

"Look!" she replied, in a whisper Nils could scarcely hear. "There—under the pines!"

Nils stared, and as he did so the beauty of the night ebbed slowly away and ancestral terrors came crawling back from exile. For beneath the trees the land was alive: a dappled brown tide was moving down the slopes of the hill and merging into the dark waters. Here was an open patch on which the moonlight fell unbroken by shadow. It was changing even as he watched: the surface of the land seemed to be rippling downward like a slow water-fall seeking union with the sea.

And then Nils laughed and the world was sane once more. Christina looked at him, puzzled but reassured.

"Don't you remember?" he chuckled. "We read all about it in the paper this morning. They do this every few years, and always at night. It's been going on for days."

He was teasing her, sweeping away the tension of the last few minutes. Christina looked back at him, and a slow smile lit up her face.

"Of course!" she said. "How stupid of me!" Then she turned once more toward the land and her expression became sad, for she was very tender-hearted.

"Poor little things!" she sighed. "I wonder why they do it?"

Nils shrugged his shoulders indifferently.

"No one knows," he answered. "It's just one of those mysteries. I shouldn't think about it if it worries you. Look—we'll soon be in harbor!"

They turned toward the beckoning lights where their future lay, and Christina glanced back only once toward the tragic, mindless tide that was still flowing beneath the moon.

Obeying an urge whose meaning they had never known, the doomed legions of the lemmings were finding oblivion beneath the waves.